SPECIAL EDITION

#15 HALLOWEIRD

Other **EERIE INDIANA** *Books*
from Avon Camelot

SPECIAL EDITION

#15 HALLOWEIRD

MIKE FORD

Based upon the television series "Eerie Indiana" created by Karl Schaefer and José Rivera

AN AVON  CAMELOT BOOK

This is a work of fiction. Names, characters, places, and incidents either are the product of the author's imagination or are used fictitiously. Any resemblance to actual events, locales, organizations, or persons, living or dead, is entirely coincidental and beyond the intent of either the author or the publisher.

AVON BOOKS, INC.
1350 Avenue of the Americas
New York, New York 10019

Copyright © 1998 by Hearst Entertainment, Inc.
Based on the Hearst Entertainment television series entitled "Eerie Indiana" created by Karl Schaefer and José Rivera
Published by arrangement with Hearst Entertainment, Inc.
Visit our website at **http://www.AvonBooks.com**
Library of Congress Catalog Card Number: 98-92789
ISBN: 0-380-80105-1

First Avon Camelot Printing: October 1998

CAMELOT TRADEMARK REG. U.S. PAT. OFF. AND IN OTHER COUNTRIES, MARCA REGISTRADA, HECHO EN U.S.A.

Printed in the U.S.A.

OPM   10   9   8   7   6   5   4   3   2   1

PROLOGUE

PROLOGUE

*M*y name is Mitchell Taylor. All my life I've lived in a small town called Eerie, Indiana. Statistically speaking, Eerie is the most normal place in the entire United States. And for the thirteen years that I've lived here, it *has* been totally normal. In fact, it's been so boring that I've begged my mom and dad to move somewhere more exciting, like New Jersey.

But not anymore. Recently something happened that made me look at my hometown in a whole new way—a way that's anything but normal.

You see, I found out that *my* Eerie, Indiana, isn't the only Eerie, Indiana. I know, it sounds really weird, right? But it's true. It seems there's this whole other dimension where there's another Eerie, Indiana, one that's a lot different from my Eerie, Indiana—or at least from the way my Eerie used to be. I still don't understand all of it, but I'm finding out more and more as the days go by.

And what I'm finding out is that practically overnight my hometown has become a very strange place to live. Underneath the perfect lawns and behind the white picket fences is a place that's crawling with unexplained stuff, and now it's my job to find the weirdness and stop it before it takes over the whole town. The only problem is that, so far, the weirdness has been finding me before I can find it.

The person who helps me battle the strangeness is my best friend and next-door neighbor, Stanley Hope. Before we discovered that we now live in the center of weirdness for the entire planet, the most excitement Stanley and I ever had was checking out the new comics at World of Stuff. Now we spend our days waiting to see what weird thing is going to happen next.

We aren't entirely on our own. We've had some help from these two kids who live in the other Eerie, Indiana, the one the weirdness came from in the first place. From what they've told us, they've been battling the weirdness for a long time.

Now it's our turn.

Still don't believe me? You will.

1

*H*alloween. Every kid's favorite time of the year, right? It's a lot of fun, but kind of spooky, too, and anything can happen. Best of all, you get to be whatever you want, at least for one night.

It used to be the holiday Stanley and I looked forward to the most. We planned our costumes months ahead of time, and on Halloween night we were the first kids to start trick-or-treating and the last kids to go home when it was all over. Then we'd take our loaded bags to my house and pour the contents all over the living-room floor. We'd turn on whatever scary movie was playing on channel 13 and watch it while we sorted through the candy and popcorn balls and gum and put everything in piles based on what we liked to eat the most. Over the next week or so, we'd eat the candy in order until nothing was left

3

but empty wrappers. Then we'd start planning for the next year.

But that was before we found out that Eerie is the center of weirdness for the entire planet. Now that we know a little bit about what's going on around here, anything the remotest bit freaky makes us a little uneasy. Ever since the weirdness leak happened between our Eerie and the other Eerie, we never know what strange thing is going to come along next, and even though we're starting to get a handle on things, we still don't really know exactly what we're dealing with.

So as the first Halloween in our newly weird hometown got closer, Stanley and I started to worry. Who wouldn't? Here we are, smack in the middle of "Weird Central," and we never know what kind of bizarre thing is going to happen next. It's not like there's some kind of weirdness alarm that goes off to warn us or anything. Usually whatever's going to happen just comes at us out of nowhere, and we have to figure out how to deal with it. There's not even a manual or anything.

Given the connection between Halloween and major weirdness, just before the thirty-first of October rolled around we held a planning session in the Secret Spot. All right, so the Secret Spot is really the attic of my house, and it's not so secret. We took the name from the place where our buddies Marshall and Simon in the other Eerie keep all of their evidence of the weirdness they've uncovered. We thought about calling it the Hideout or the Headquarters or something, but nothing sounded quite as good.

Anyway, like I said, the Secret Spot is really the attic of my house. No one ever really uses it for anything, so when Stanley and I became investigators of the strange and unusual, we just sort of moved in. Now it's really cool up there. We have a desk and a cabinet to keep all of our files in. We also have a trunk where we keep the evidence we collect. I moved my computer up there, and we even have some sleeping bags so that when Stanley stays over we can hold top-secret discussions about the weirdness that has taken over Eerie.

That's what we were doing on the afternoon of Sunday, October 28. We'd told my mother that we were working on a project for school, but really we were up in the Secret Spot comparing notes about potential weirdness.

"Nothing new at school," said Stanley, who is a couple of years behind me and keeps his eye on the kids in his grade while I watch the ones in my class. "Mrs. Twister has been teaching us about cloning in science class, but that's no big deal."

"Great," I said, writing his observation down in a notebook we record evidence in. "But if she asks for volunteers to help her with her experiments, then there could be trouble. Keep an eye on her."

"Right," agreed Stanley. "How about you—anything new to report?"

"So far, so good," I answered. "Everything seems to be going as usual. The ninth grade is holding the Halloween dance like they do every year. The cheerleaders are having their big pumpkin bake sale on Wednesday. Oh, and that will also be Costume Day at school. So we should think of what we want to be. But that's about it. No strange lights over the town. No unexplained disappearances. Nothing freaky showing up in the sewers. Everything is perfectly normal."

Stanley thought for a minute. "Yeah, but isn't *that* weird?" he asked. "You know, it's weird that nothing's weird. Ever since the rip in the dimensional wall, there's always been *something* weird going on. Now it's dead."

"I was sort of hoping the weirdness was taking a break," I said. "Like maybe it went on vacation for Halloween or something. You'd think even

6

weirdness would want some time off every now and then."

"Maybe," said Stanley. "It would be nice to enjoy Halloween without worrying about something popping up."

"What do you want to go as this year?" I asked.

Stanley groaned. "I don't know. I keep thinking of things that would be cool. Then I remember that a lot of those things are probably actually running around Eerie somewhere, and I get all freaked about it."

"I know what you mean," I said. "The other night I walked past Kari's room and thought a wolfman was attacking her. I ran in to save her and just about scared her to death. It was just a mask she had hanging on her closet doorknob. But I thought it was real."

"Maybe we shouldn't go as anything," suggested Stanley. "We could just stay home."

"We can't do that," I said. "It's Halloween. The coolest night of the year." I tried to sound enthusiastic, even though the truth was that I was thinking the same thing Stanley was. If the weirdness was going to give us a night off, I wanted to take it.

Before we could talk about it anymore, there was a knock on the door to the Secret Spot.

"Come in," I called.

The door opened and my father walked in.

"Hey, guys," he said. "Planning your Halloween costumes?"

"Not exactly," I said.

"Well," my dad said. "I just need to look in some boxes over here for a minute."

Even though the Secret Spot was Stanley's and my hideout, it was still the attic, and there was some attic-type stuff in there. My father walked over to some old cardboard boxes and started moving them around.

"What are you looking for?" I asked, watching as my dad opened a box and began to rummage through it.

"Oh, just an old book," my dad said. "Some of the guys at the station and I are planning a Halloween show."

My dad teaches science at Eerie University, but he also has a part-time job at radio station WERD. It's not even really a job. More like a hobby. He hosts a radio show where he plays music and talks about stuff he thinks is interesting. Only usually he's the only one who would call it interesting. The rest of us call it, well . . . boring.

"What kind of show?" asked Stanley. "Creepy music or something?"

"Even better," said my dad. "We're going to do

a broadcast of *War of the Worlds.* Only I'm going to rewrite it so that it takes place in Eerie. But I need to find my copy of it. It's in here somewhere."

Stanley looked at me with a strange expression. "What's *War of the Worlds?*" he asked.

I shook my head. "Never heard of it."

My father turned around. "You guys have never heard of *War of the Worlds?* I thought you were both into scary stuff."

"Yeah, well, there's a lot more to learn than we thought," I said. "We must have missed that. So what is it?"

My dad pulled something out of the box. Then he came over and sat down on one of the beds. He waved a battered copy of a book at us. On the cover there was a picture of a woman running from what looked like a flying saucer with octopus-like tentacles coming out of it.

"This is *War of the Worlds,*" he said.

"It's an old book?" I said.

He sighed. "No, it's not just an old book. It was a radio show. More important, it was the single most frightening thing ever to be aired on the radio."

"What's so scary about radio?" said Stanley. "It's just a bunch of people talking in between songs."

"It didn't used to be like that," said my father. "Radio used to be really exciting. And nothing was more exciting than this particular radio broadcast."

"All right, already," I said. "We get the idea. So what's so special about this show?"

My father looked at us both. Then he said excitedly, "On October 30, 1938, one of the greatest radio broadcasters of all time—Orson Welles—put on *The War of the Worlds*. It's the story of a small town invaded by Martians."

"Sounds kind of silly," I said. "What was the big deal?"

"The big deal is that Welles's broadcast sounded exactly like a news bulletin," my father continued. "People who tuned in and didn't know it was a radio show thought it was really a live report about aliens invading New Jersey."

"Why would aliens want to go to New Jersey?" asked Stanley.

"That doesn't matter," said my dad. "What matters is that millions of people across the country believed it was actually happening. They really thought the United States was being invaded by creatures from Mars. They panicked, and there was mass hysteria. People tried to leave New York City because they thought the aliens were heading there next. People locked themselves in their cellars and barricaded their houses. Some stormed police stations demanding protection from the aliens. All over America, search parties went out looking for Martians. It was the biggest hoax in the history of modern communications."

"And you want to do the show here?" I said, feeling a little frightened. "That doesn't sound too smart."

"It's a classic," said my father. "Nowadays, everyone knows it isn't real. I want to rewrite it so that the aliens aren't landing in New Jersey—they're landing right here in Eerie. It will be fantastic—a return to radio the way it used to be. We're going to air it live on Halloween night. Hey, I bet I could write in some parts for you two. What do you say?"

"Um . . . that's okay, Dad," I said. "Stanley and I have other plans for Halloween night."

"Suit yourselves," my father said. "I'm going to take this downstairs and get started on rewriting it. I only have a couple of days."

My father disappeared down the stairs, leaving Stanley and me alone again.

"That show sounds kind of strange," said Stanley. "Can you imagine all those people really believing that aliens were invading New Jersey?"

I laughed. "That's fine for people in New Jersey," I said. "But I don't think anybody in Eerie is going to fall for it. Here, people don't even believe all of the weird things that are happening right under their noses."

"We still haven't decided what to do about Halloween," said Stanley. "We told your dad we had plans, but we don't."

"I know," I said. "We'd better come up with something, or else he'll make us be in his show."

"There's a new costume shop that just opened up downtown," said Stanley. "It's called the Monster Factory. I saw an ad for it in the paper this morning. Maybe we should go check it out and see if we can come up with any ideas on what to be."

"Good idea," I said. "If we wait too long, we'll end up going as something dorky, like ghosts or football players."

We left the Secret Spot and headed for the front door of my house. As we passed my father's office, I saw him tapping at the computer keyboard and humming to himself.

" 'Bye, Dad," I called out. "Stanley and I are going into town for a little while. We'll be back before dinner."

"Great," he said, typing away. "Have a good time."

Stanley and I grabbed our jackets and left the

house. Outside, the October air was crisp and cold. All along the street, the trees were covered in leaves colored red, yellow, and orange. Some of the trees had already lost their leaves, and their thin branches stuck up black and spiky against the blue sky. As we shuffled along, kicking at the piles of fallen leaves that lined the sidewalk, we both stuffed our hands into our pockets to keep them warm.

"Remember how much fun Halloween was last year?" I said to Stanley as we walked past houses decorated with paper skeletons, grinning witches, and black cats.

"Yeah," said Stanley. "That gargoyle costume you made out of chicken wire and papier-mâché was great."

"Your two-headed zombie wasn't so bad, either," I said. "And don't forget, we both tied for first place at the school dance."

Stanley sighed. "This year I don't even feel like carving a jack-o'-lantern," he said. "Just looking at them gives me the creeps."

We were passing a house that had not one but three carved pumpkins on the porch. Their grinning mouths and weird triangular eyes had never seemed scary to me before, but now that I knew what kind of weirdness was lurking beneath Eerie's streets, just looking at the jack-o'-lanterns made a chill run down my spine.

"We can't let it get to us," I said. "We're going to have a good time. Remember, Marshall and Simon told us that the best way to fight the weirdness is to not be afraid of it."

"Easier said than done," said Stanley as we turned onto Main Street.

Halloween has always been a favorite time in Eerie, and every store we passed was decorated for the holiday. The grocery store had a display of gourds that looked like goblin heads. The pet store had a tank filled with tarantulas in the front window. The bookstore was advertising a series of readings of scary books, just for Halloween.

"Wow," said Stanley as we passed the bookstore. "M. T. Coffin is going to be reading there tomorrow night. I love his Spinetingler books. We should go."

"Costumes first," I said, steering him away from the bookstore and down the street.

"There it is," said Stanley. He was pointing to a store on the corner. It was right next to the florist shop, which was having a half-price sale on Venus's flytraps.

When we pushed open the door of the Monster Factory, someone let out a horrible scream.

"What was that?" I shouted, looking around to see what had happened.

"It's nothing to be afraid of," called a voice from the back of the store. "It's just the doorbell."

A figure emerged from behind a rack of costumes, pushing aside a tiger suit and a fairy godmother dress and stepping out into the room. It was an elderly woman. She had lots of gray hair, and it was piled up in a bun that seemed in danger of sliding right off her head if she moved too quickly. Her skin was very wrinkled, and she was wearing an apron, the pockets of which were overflowing with things like needles and thread, a tape measure, and all kinds of pencils.

"Welcome to the Monster Factory," she said. "I'm the owner, Mrs. Crisp."

"Do you make all of these costumes?" I asked, looking around. The entire store was crammed with suits, masks, feathers, props, and all kinds of things for Halloween outfits.

"Indeed I do," Mrs. Crisp said. "For years I was a costume designer for a theater company. When I retired, I decided to try my hand at Halloween costumes."

"What brought you to Eerie?" asked Stanley.

Mrs. Crisp cocked her head. Even though she was clearly very old, her eyes were a sparkling shade of blue. In fact, they were almost *too* blue, like someone had dyed them and used too much coloring.

"I was just drawn here," she said. "I looked all over for the perfect place to open my shop. I happened to be traveling through Eerie, and I just loved it. It's perfect for what I want to do."

"And what's that?" I asked her as I started to look through the racks of costumes.

Mrs. Crisp laughed. "Why, I want to make Halloween a night no one in Eerie will ever forget," she said as she came over and helped me look. "Now, why don't we find you the perfect costume?"

As I looked at Mrs. Crisp's smiling face, I began to think that maybe Halloween was going to be okay after all.

I thought wrong.

2

Mrs. Crisp worked her way through the first rack of costumes quickly. Every so often she pulled one out and held it up to me to see how it looked. Stepping back, she would eye me up and down, but every time she would end up shaking her head and putting the costume back. She tried a clown suit, a vampire, a knight, and even a giant peanut costume, but none of them looked right to her.

"This calls for something extra special," she said when she reached the end of the rack without finding anything. "I can tell you're a young man who likes the out of the ordinary. Am I right?"

I nodded. "Sure," I said. "I don't want to be like everybody else. I want my costume to stand out."

"Mm-hmm," said Mrs. Crisp as she thought for a minute. Then her face lit up. "I've got it!" she said. "There's something I've been saving for a special occasion. I think it will be perfect for you."

She dashed into the back of the store, moving a lot more quickly than I would expect an elderly woman to. Then I heard a crash.

"What was that?" Stanley asked.

I shook my head. "Are you all right back there?" I shouted. "Do you need any help?"

"No, thank you, dear," Mrs. Crisp shouted back. "I'm just taking down some boxes, and one fell on the floor. It's quite all right."

There were more rustling sounds, and then what sounded like a big trash can being dragged across the floor. I looked at Stanley.

"Sounds like it's going to be some costume," I said. "I wonder what it is."

Just then, Mrs. Crisp came bustling back into the room. She was carrying what looked like an ancient deep-sea diving helmet. The front—the part that would cover the face—had a round piece of glass, and there were all kinds of hoses attached to it. On one side there was an attachment that looked like a camera lens.

"What's that?" I asked when she held it up for me to see.

"One of my best creations," she said. "It's an exact replica of a Martian environmental exploration breathing apparatus."

"A Martian *what?*" asked Stanley.

"An alien space helmet," said Mrs. Crisp.

Stanley gave me a funny look.

"I mean, it's what I imagine an alien space helmet would look like," she said when she saw us sneaking glances at each other. "I worked mainly in theater, but I did some costume designing for films as well. I once worked on a space picture."

"It must have been a very old picture," I said as I took the helmet from her. "This thing looks prehistoric."

"Well, it was quite a long time ago," she said. "The movie was called *The Day They Came*. It was all about Martians landing on Earth."

"That makes two alien landings I've never heard of," I said, thinking about my father and his story about *War of the Worlds*.

"Excuse me?" asked Mrs. Crisp as she fit the helmet over my head.

"Nothing," I replied, my voice echoing inside the helmet. "It's just that you're the second person today who has mentioned Martians landing."

"Really?" asked Mrs. Crisp. She sounded very interested. "Who was the other person?"

"Just my dad," I said as I tried moving around with the helmet on. "He's a little out of this world anyway."

Mrs. Crisp smiled. "I see," she said. "By the way, what did you say your names were?"

"We didn't," said Stanley. "But I'm Stanley, and the guy playing astronaut is Mitchell."

"Well, Mitchell, what do you think of the helmet?" asked Mrs. Crisp.

"It's really cool," I said. And it was. It took a little while to get used to looking through the camera attachment, but otherwise the helmet was great. I felt like a real space explorer as I wandered around the shop.

"Hey, what are all of these lights flashing around in here?" I asked as a series of blue numbers and letters began to scroll across the lower edge of the eyepiece.

"Oh, just ignore those," said Mrs. Crisp. "Those are just random readouts. It's a special effect the movie director wanted."

"Well, they're pretty neat," I said. "Even if they don't mean anything."

"Just out of curiosity," said Mrs. Crisp, "what kind of readout do you get when you look at Stanley?"

I turned around and looked at Stanley. As the eyepiece focused on him, a red horizontal line appeared. Then the line began to shift downward. It started at Stanley's head and moved down his body, like it was scanning him.

"This is really far-out," I said. "It's like the scanner at the supermarket that reads the bar codes on food."

As the red line moved down Stanley's body, a line of numbers scrolled across the bottom of the eyepiece. None of them meant anything to me. But when the line reached his feet, the numbers began to fly by more rapidly, and then the word *human* flashed on and off where the numbers were before.

"It just says 'human'," I said to Mrs. Crisp.

She nodded. "Good," she said. "That's what it's supposed to do. Sometimes the program chip gets a little weird and it spits out something different. If it should do that while you're wearing it, don't worry. It doesn't mean it's broken or anything."

"It's great," I said. "But I don't think I can afford it."

Mrs. Crisp waved her hand at me. "Don't even think about it," she said. "Consider it a loan from me. Besides, it's up to you to make the rest of the costume. I'm just giving you the helmet."

"Wow," I said. "Thanks a lot. I can make something really cool out of this."

"That takes care of you, then," said Mrs. Crisp. "Now what shall we do for your friend?"

"Me?" asked Stanley hopefully.

"Of course," said Mrs. Crisp. "We can't have

Mitchell here being the only one with a Halloween costume that's out of this world."

"What could I be?" asked Stanley.

Mrs. Crisp looked at him for a minute, then she went to a rack at the back of the store and flipped through the costumes. When she came back she was carrying a strange-looking rubber head. It looked like a big fish head, only it was a weird reddish color, and some of the scales on the fish were painted bright colors. It also had enormous eyes, and the mouth was open like the fish was gasping for air.

"How do you like this?" asked Mrs. Crisp as she held the head up.

"That's amazing!" exclaimed Stanley. "A giant fish!"

"Not exactly," said Mrs. Crisp. "A Karakian moon guppy."

"What?" asked Stanley and I together.

"From the Sea of Karakia on the moon of Pluto," said Mrs. Crisp. "Honestly, don't you boys watch science fiction movies? It's one of the characters from *Battle of the Spacefish.*"

"We must have missed that one," said Stanley as he took the fish head from Mrs. Crisp.

The mask went over Stanley's own head and rested on his shoulders. Only the fake head was a lot bigger than his real one, so the eye holes were actually in the fish's mouth, while the eyes on the mask were somewhere above Stanley's hair.

"Can you see all right?" asked Mrs. Crisp as she adjusted the mask a little.

Stanley nodded, and the giant fish head bobbed up and down. It looked really weird, especially because when I looked down I saw Stanley's familiar jeans and tennis shoes.

"This is really wild," said Stanley, turning and looking at himself in a mirror. "I feel like a real fish."

"It's a perfect fit," said Mrs. Crisp, clapping her hands together. "When I saw the two of you, I just knew I'd have something that would be perfect for you."

"You were sure right," said Stanley, pulling the fish head off. "These couldn't be better."

"Are you sure you don't want us to pay for them?" I asked. "I feel bad just taking them."

Mrs. Crisp smiled. "I make the costumes because I like to, dear," she said. "I don't need the money. But if you want to do something for me, there is something I could use some help with."

"Sure," said Stanley. "Anything you want, we can do. I mean, it's not every Halloween you get to be a Karakian moon guppy and a Martian explorer."

"Well," said Mrs. Crisp. "It's really very silly. But it would mean a great deal to me. You see, I'd like to have a parade."

"A parade?" I asked. "What kind of parade?"

"A Halloween parade," said Mrs. Crisp. "Being new in Eerie, I'd like to do something for my new hometown. And since I like costumes so much, I thought I might organize a big Halloween parade and party on the lawn in front of the town hall."

"That sounds like fun," said Stanley. "You could have bobbing for apples and stuff like that."

"Exactly," said Mrs. Crisp. "Oh, that would be so much fun. I do love a good parade. So, will you help me?"

Stanley looked at me, and I shrugged. "Why not?" I said. "Nothing else much happens around here on Halloween. I bet people would really enjoy that."

"Good," said Mrs. Crisp. "But we don't have a lot of time. Halloween is Wednesday night. We have a great deal of work to do. Can you boys come over tomorrow after school and help me get started?"

"I guess we can," I said.

"I'll have to get busy making plans, then," said Mrs. Crisp. "You boys take those costumes home and put them somewhere safe. We don't want anyone running off with them or anything."

"We will," said Stanley as we walked to the door. "And we'll be back tomorrow."

As we walked back to my house with our masks under our arms, we were a lot happier than we were on the way into town. For some reason, all of the negative feelings I'd been having about Halloween were gone. I wasn't worried about what might go wrong. Instead, I was looking forward to it.

"It's so cool of Mrs. Crisp to let us use these," I said, holding my spaceman helmet tightly.

"You're telling me?" said Stanley. "No one is going to have costumes like these. No one. And this Halloween parade is going to be great. Now we don't have to worry about being on the lookout for weirdness all night. What can happen at a parade?"

We went back to my house and took our costumes up into the Secret Spot. Even though we had the masks, we still had to come up with the rest of our outfits, so I asked if Stanley could stay for dinner. Both of our moms said it was okay, so he got to experience my mother's infamous Sunday Night Meatloaf. My mother makes this every Sunday night, and it consists of hamburger plus whatever else happens to be left in the refrigerator from the week before.

On this particular night, the meatloaf had

pieces of macaroni and cheese from Wednesday night in it, along with some peas from Thursday and a little bit of Friday's mashed potatoes. It looked really weird, and I was amazed when Stanley ate four helpings.

"We never have anything like this at my house," he said. "My mom always orders out."

"Next time we'll eat over at your house," I said as I picked at my meatloaf and held up a forkful of unidentifiable food. "What is this, spinach from yesterday?"

"It's good for you," my mother said. "Now eat up. We have tapioca pudding for dessert."

"Ugh," I said. "That stuff looks like fish eyes in glue."

Stanley, of course, turned out to love tapioca almost as much as the mystery meatloaf. Kari and I were both happy to give him our own servings, and watched in amazement as he wolfed them down.

"Sometimes I think you must come from another planet," said Kari as Stanley licked the last bits of tapioca out of his bowl.

"Speaking of coming from another planet," my father said, putting down his spoon, "I have to get back to my script. I'm almost done with my version of *War of the Worlds*. Would anyone care to hear a dramatic reading of it later on?"

"Sorry," said Kari. "Brittany and I have a phone date."

"To talk about the crucial issue of what to wear to school tomorrow, no doubt," I said.

"No," said Kari. "If you must know, it's so we can plan what we're making for the bake sale on Wednesday. She's coming here Tuesday night and we're going to make something."

"Uh-oh," I said. "Cheerleaders in the kitchen. You'd better alert the fire department, Mom. The last time Kari tried to cook, every smoke alarm in the house went off."

"Fine," said Kari. "We'll just see if I give you any of my famous chocolate-chip cookies. At least I'm doing something to celebrate the spirit of Halloween. That's more than I can say for you two."

"Don't count on it," I said. "Stanley and I just happen to be involved in the biggest Halloween surprise to hit Eerie since the invention of the snack-size candy bar."

"And just what would that be?" my mother asked.

"We can't say just yet," I said, grinning. "But you'll know soon enough."

"Well, if no one wants to hear my play, then I guess I'll just go read it to myself," my father said with fake sadness.

"I'm sure it's wonderful, Edward," said my mother. "We can't wait to hear it on the radio."

"Right," said Kari.

"Sure," said Stanley and I.

"Okay, then," said my dad, and he went off to his office.

Stanley and I cleared the table, then ran upstairs to the Secret Spot. I shut the door, and we tried on our Halloween masks again and looked in the mirror. We really did look fantastic, like two characters straight out of *Star Wars* or something.

"We have to come up with some great costumes to go with these," said Stanley when we took our masks off.

"I think there's some cool stuff in these boxes of old clothes," I said, going over to the part of the attic where my mother had stored some things.

I opened one of the boxes, and Stanley and I started looking through it. I found a white jumpsuit that looked like a spacesuit and tried it on.

"Perfect," said Stanley. "You look just like some kind of alien bounty hunter or something."

"Get in the spaceship or I'll have to use this," I said jokingly, pointing a hairbrush like a ray gun.

Stanley pulled something out of the box. It was a long bathrobe made out of some kind of purple silky material. He put it on and tied the belt around his waist. The robe was a little big, and it billowed out around him.

"Excellent," I said once he'd put on the fish head. "It looks exactly like something a Karakian moon guppy would wear. You know, if fish wore clothes."

Stanley marched around the room, perfecting his Karakian moon guppy walk, while I found some other things in the box to add to my costume.

"These costumes beat anything ever seen in Eerie," said Stanley.

"Yeah," I said as I took a thick leather belt out of the box and started to fasten it around my waist. "We're going to knock them dead. What do you think of this?"

There was no answer.

"Stanley?" I said. "I asked you what you think—"

"I think you need to take a look at this," said Stanley in a strange voice.

"Take a look at what?" I asked, turning around.

Stanley was standing at the window, looking out at the night sky. I walked over and looked out, too. I didn't see anything.

"What's the big deal?" I asked.

"Over there," said Stanley, pointing.

I followed his finger. Out past the edge of town,

near the abandoned railroad yard, something was hovering in the sky. It was round and orange, and it glowed dimly in the darkness.

As Stanley and I watched, the orange thing circled slowly in the air. Then it started to glow a little bit brighter, filling up with light until it was glowing like a hot coal. Then, all of a sudden, it shot straight up into the sky and just disappeared, like a light winking out.

"What was it?" I asked, staring at the empty black sky where the thing had been a moment before.

"I don't know," said Stanley. "And I don't think I want to know."

3

"Oh, man," I said as I sank into my chair. "I thought we were through with the weirdness for a little while."

"Nobody said anything about weirdness," said Stanley. "For all we know, there's a perfectly reasonable explanation for whatever that was. Like maybe it was a searchlight or something."

"Searchlights aren't orange, and they don't shoot up into the sky like that," I said.

"Okay," admitted Stanley. "So maybe someone was shooting off fireworks."

"Uh-uh."

"Swamp gas?" Stanley suggested.

I shook my head.

"Weather balloon?" he tried weakly.

"No," I said, facing the truth. "It was definitely weirdness. The question is, what kind of weirdness?"

"Why do we have to find out?" asked Stanley, flopping down on the old couch. "Why can't we just leave it alone? Isn't there some kind of rule that we only have to worry about the weirdness when it comes to us? No one ever said we had to go out looking for it."

"It's our duty to investigate any weirdness we encounter," I reminded him. "We owe it to Marshall and Simon. I bet they'd already be out there looking for clues."

"Yeah, well, we aren't them," said Stanley. "We didn't ask them to send the weirdness over here."

"It wasn't their fault," I said.

Stanley sighed. "I know. I just wanted this week to be—you know—normal. I was looking forward to Halloween and all."

I patted Stanley on the back. "Hey, who says it still won't be normal? For all we know, this is nothing big. But we do have to check it out. Remember—we're the defenders of Eerie, Indiana."

"I think it's time for a new job," Stanley grumbled as he stood up.

"Look on the bright side," I said, pointing to our costumes. "At least we have these cool outfits."

Quickly we changed back into our normal clothes, put on our jackets, and grabbed our backpacks from the closet. After our first adventures we'd learned the importance of being prepared for anything, so we always keep our packs filled with all the things we might need on a weirdness mission, including flashlights, cameras, walkie-talkies, and pocketknives. That way, we're always ready to go in case of an emergency.

I told my mother that we were going over to Stanley's for a little while to work on some homework, then we went out the front door.

"That light was somewhere over by the old train yard," I said. "That's quite a ways. We should take the bikes."

We went to the garage and got the bikes out. Hopping on, we pedaled down the street and turned onto the road that led out toward the abandoned train yard. A long time ago, Eerie was a major stop on the railway line. But the trains stopped running years back, and now what's left of the old yard sits there, rotting away. Sometimes kids go out there to play on the rusted-out trains, but most people stay away from it.

The road out to the yard is really just a bumpy dirt track, and our bikes bounced and clattered along as we made our way through the night. The overgrown weeds along the side of the road swayed in the wind, and it felt like we were riding into the middle of nowhere as we wound along the twists and turns of the abandoned track. Finally, the path grew steeper as we climbed the small hill that overlooked the train yard. Then the looming shadows of the wrecked trains and the old yard buildings came into view, and we came to a stop.

"Well, here we are," said Stanley as we looked down at the rotting buildings.

In the darkness, the old train yard was really spooky. The main depot, where the trains used to stop to let people on and off, sat in the middle of the lot. It was a big building with old-fashioned windows that were boarded up and a door that was locked with a huge padlock. All kinds of signs warning people to stay out and not to trespass were plastered on the peeling walls.

Around the yard, the thin metal rails of the train tracks stretched out like ribbons of metal shining dully in the moonlight. The land around the tracks was bare dirt, and the tracks looked almost like scars stretched over dry skin. Here and there, old train cars sat silently, abandoned long ago. Some had their windows broken and graffiti sprayed on their sides. Others had sunk into the ground on one side, so that they looked like big metal animals lurching around, and their dark doorways looked like mouths.

"It doesn't look like anything is going on," said

Stanley after we'd looked at the yard for a minute. "Maybe we should just go."

Stanley sounded scared. I knew just how he felt. Something about looking at that place, which used to be filled with so many people and had so much going on but was now deserted and falling apart, made me feel really creepy. It was almost like everyone had just disappeared, leaving the empty train cars and dilapidated buildings behind.

"No," I said. "We can't leave. We have to look around."

I pushed my bike over the top of the hill and coasted down the other side into the train yard. Stanley followed behind me. As we rolled through the rows of train skeletons, I scanned the area for any signs of weirdness. But in the dark everything looked a little weird, and I had no idea what I was looking for.

We rode our bikes along a set of tracks that didn't have any abandoned train cars on it. I guess neither one of us wanted to be too close to the trains, in case someone—or something—was waiting inside to give us a surprise.

The tracks led toward a clear area of the yard where a number of other tracks converged in a big circle. It was where the trains used to pull in and turn around to start their journeys away from Eerie and back to wherever it was they came from. The metal circle looked like the center of a spider web, with the tracks forming the lines that spun out from it.

In the opening formed by the circle was a bare area of dirt. Little patches of dried grass stuck up from the ground, which was littered with old soda cans, pieces of crumpled paper, and bits of broken glass that glittered in the moonlight like thousands of tiny eyes. It looked a lot like the ground in any old lot that no one takes care of.

But something wasn't quite right about the ground. It looked too dark, even at night. I got off my bike and went over to get a closer look. After stepping across the edge of the tracks, I knelt down to examine the ground. I touched it, then pulled my hand back.

"It's hot!" I said to Stanley, who was standing next to me, shining his flashlight around.

"What do you mean, it's hot?" he asked.

"The ground," I said. "When I touched it. It's so hot that it almost burned me."

I turned my hand over to see if my palm was scorched. It still felt hot. But when I saw the skin, I almost fainted. It was pitch black.

For a moment I thought that I'd burned myself really badly. Then I realized that it would hurt if I had, and it didn't. I reached out with my other hand and poked at my palm. Some of the blackness rubbed away.

"It's just dirt," I said, wiping my hand on my pants.

"No, it isn't," said Stanley. He was kneeling down and touching the earth. He took one finger and drew a line in the dirt. "See, it's not dirt. It's soot."

"You mean, like something was burned here?" I asked.

He nodded. "The whole circle is burnt," he said. "It's like someone had a big bonfire or something. That must be what the orange ball we saw was. Well, at least it was something normal."

"But there are no charred logs," I said. "Besides, someone would have seen a fire this big." I knew that sometimes older kids came to the train yard to hold bonfires, but usually only in the summer. And no fire big enough to burn the whole circle would burn for long. The fire department would be out there in a minute to put it out.

Stanley followed the circle of train tracks with his flashlight.

"Come look at this," he called when he reached the far side.

I ran around the tracks and stopped beside him. He was shining the flashlight along the ground leading away from the circle.

"What is it?" I asked, trying to see what he was looking at.

"The ground," he said, pointing.

The ground wasn't burnt like the ground inside the circle, but there was definitely something on it. Every foot or so there was a strange depression in the dirt. Each dent was shaped like a circle with three long lines sticking out from it. There was a line of marks running in one direction, and another line running in the opposite direction.

"They look like footprints," I said.

"Right," said Stanley. "One set going away from the circle and one set coming back."

"But what makes footprints like that?" I asked. "They certainly aren't human, and they don't look like any animal I've ever seen."

"There's only one way to find out," said Stanley, nodding in the direction of the footprints. "They go that way." The beam of his flashlight cut through the darkness, flooding the side of the old train depot with light. The footprints headed right for it.

"What if it's still there?" I asked. "Anything that could burn the ground like that will be awfully big."

"Great," said Stanley. "Next you're going to tell me there's a dragon waiting in there for us."

"This is Eerie," I said as I started walking toward the depot. "It could be anything."

We followed the weird footprints, shining our flashlights around us as we walked. But aside from the prints and the strange circle of burned ground we'd left behind, nothing was unusual.

When we got close to the old depot, we saw that the tracks veered around toward the side of the building. We followed them, and were surprised when they ended at a solid wall. The tracks just stopped. There were no doors, no windows, and no way into the place.

"Now it's officially weird," said Stanley, looking at the wall. "Maybe whatever made these tracks just turned around and went back."

"That doesn't make any sense," I said. "Why would it walk to this spot and then go back? If it really wanted to get inside, it could try to get in through a window or something."

The brick wall of the depot was covered with spray paint, and the few windows that were still left were either broken or covered with grime. There were a few old posters stuck to the wall as well. Mostly they were old advertisements for products like Eerie Orchard apple juice and Ever Pure soap. The pictures were all faded, and most of the posters were torn in places.

Right above the spot where the footprints

stopped was a poster that looked a little newer than the other ones. It was a big sheet of paper with a picture of a smiling woman on it. She was drinking something from a bottle, and across the top of the poster a slogan read: DRINK EERIE COLA! IT'S OUT OF THIS WORLD!

"I've never heard of Eerie Cola," I said as I looked at the poster more carefully. "Have you?"

"No," said Stanley. "Maybe they don't make it anymore."

I reached out to touch the poster. I thought it might be cool to hang it in the Secret Spot, and I wanted to see if I could peel it off. But when I touched it, my hand went right through and into the wall.

"Hey!" I exclaimed, and pulled my hand back. "Did you see that?"

"Yeah," said Stanley. "What just happened?"

"I don't know," I said. "My hand just went into the wall."

"Did it hurt?" asked Stanley.

"No," I said. "It didn't feel like anything."

I reached my hand out again and poked at the poster. The tip of my finger sank into the woman's cheek and disappeared. This time, I didn't pull back. I pushed a little more and watched as my whole hand, and then my wrist, went into the brick.

"What is it?" asked Stanley, staring at my arm.

"There's only one way to find out," I said.

Stanley grabbed my arm. "Don't!" he said. "Don't you remember what happened with the TV set and the rip in the dimensional wall? You could end up somewhere and never be able to get back."

"I don't think this is like that," I told him. "It doesn't feel the same. You just wait here. I'll be right back."

"You'd better be," said Stanley. "How would I explain to your mom that you disappeared into some cola woman's head?"

I pushed into the wall and felt myself sliding through. It didn't feel like anything, really. One second I was outside and the next I wasn't.

But where I was wasn't exactly clear. I was inside the train depot—that much I knew. Only it wasn't the falling-down wreck of a depot that it should have been. It was a completely restored train station, just like it would have looked fifty years before, when it was in use. The ceiling soared above me, it's decorations painted bright gold. There were rows of polished wooden benches and giant potted plants. Under my feet was a shiny marble floor that stretched across the lobby of the train station and ended at a row of gleaming ticket windows. Each window had a shade pulled down and a CLOSED sign hanging behind the glass.

Turning around, I saw that I had just walked through a big revolving door. It looked like any big glass door in an old train station, but the glass was frosted and I couldn't see outside. I put my hand on the glass and pushed. The door swung around, I went through, and I found myself once more standing in the cold October night. Stanley was staring at me and blowing on his hands.

"Well?" he said.

"It's hard to explain," I said. "Follow me."

I took Stanley's hand. This time I just went right through the poster, pulling Stanley with me.

"What's the big deal?" he asked when we were standing once more inside the depot. His eyes were closed.

"Open your eyes," I said. "Whatever you're expecting, this isn't it."

Stanley opened one eye and looked around. When he saw where we were, he opened his other eye and just stood there, staring at everything.

"But . . ." he said. "How . . . ? I mean . . . Where? I mean, What's going on here?"

"You got me," I said.

Just then, a door opened on the other side of

the depot and someone walked through. It was a man. He was dressed in an old-fashioned uniform, and wore a hat like a train conductor's. He was looking at a pocket watch. When he looked up and saw us, he frowned.

"What are you doing here?" he asked, walking toward us. "There isn't supposed to be an arrival for another three hours."

I didn't know what the man was talking about or who he was, but I got the feeling that Stanley and I would be in big trouble if he knew where we'd come from.

"Um, we're a little early?" I said timidly, hoping he'd buy it.

"I didn't hear any landing," the man said. "What ship did you come in on?"

I looked at Stanley. I didn't know what to say.

"Oh, we came in on the excursion train from Barstow," said Stanley, making something up.

"What?" asked the man. "Who *are* you two?"

We were in trouble. Whoever the man was, and whatever was going on, we weren't supposed to be there.

"We have to go now," I said. Then I turned to Stanley. "Run!" I shouted.

We bolted for the revolving door.

"Come back here!" bellowed the man, and lunged at us.

Luckily, he missed and ended up sprawled on the marble floor just as Stanley and I reached the door. I could see him starting to get up as I pushed on the glass and the door spun around. Then I was flying through the air and landing on the ground back in the train yard.

4

Stanley landed next to me a second later. I heard him gasp as he hit the ground and rolled onto his back to catch his breath. Behind us, the wall was just a wall again, and the Eerie Cola ad looked like a perfectly ordinary poster.

"We'd better get out of here," I said to Stanley. "That guy's probably after us."

Stanley and I scrambled to our feet and ran around the side of the train depot, back to where we'd left our bikes. We jumped on and pedaled back up the hill, our shaky legs moving as fast as they could go. We didn't even look back as we tore down the dirt path back to the main road. If anyone was following us, we didn't want to get caught there. For the first time, I thought how stupid it was for us to be running around without anyone knowing where we were.

When we reached the solid surface of the paved

road, we hightailed it back into town, putting as much distance as we could between us and the train yard. We didn't stop until we screeched to a halt in front of my house. Only then did we look back to make sure we were alone. The road was empty, and all we heard was the sound of the wind blowing a few leaves along the sidewalk.

"What just happened back there?" Stanley asked, breaking the silence. "One second we're standing in front of an abandoned train station, and the next we're inside the station. Only it isn't abandoned anymore, and some guy is asking us which ship we came in on. And since when are there *ships* at a *train* station, anyway?"

I didn't have any answers for Stanley. All I knew was that what had just happened was real. I hadn't dreamed it. I looked down at my pants and saw the black soot stains there, and I could tell I was going to have a nasty bruise on my arm from landing on the ground.

"We're not going to find out anything more tonight," was all I could say. "All we have now are more questions."

"I told you we shouldn't have gone out there," said Stanley. "I knew we should have just stayed up in the Secret Spot where it's nice and safe and walls are walls and nothing weird ever happens."

"Sure," I said. "We could have stayed up there.

But we didn't. And you have to admit, it was pretty cool."

Stanley stared at me for a moment. Then he grinned. "Yeah," he said, "it was pretty neat. If I hadn't been so scared, I might have actually liked it."

We both laughed. Then we put the bikes back in my garage and said good night, after agreeing to meet in the morning to walk to school. I went inside and up to my room, where I lay down and thought about everything that had happened. Despite my joking around with Stanley, I was worried. We'd encountered some strange things since Ted Tanner's satellite dishes first turned Eerie into the center of weirdness for the entire planet. But somehow this seemed bigger than our other problems. I didn't know why, but something told me that there was more going on inside the freaky train depot than just some guy walking around asking for tickets.

There wasn't, however, anything I could do about it at the moment. Whatever kind of weirdness was running around that night, it would still be there in the morning. I turned off my light and went to sleep.

When I woke up, the first thing I remembered wasn't the night before, but that I had a science test that I hadn't studied for. All thoughts of the strange train station went right out of my head as I quickly got dressed, grabbed my books, and ran downstairs. After wolfing down a glass of juice and a doughnut, I ran out of the house. Stanley was waiting for me.

"I think I figured it out," he said as I came running up.

"No time!" I said. "I have to get to school and study for a few minutes."

"But Mitch, I figured it out!" he said as I kept running.

"Great," I said, ignoring him as I flipped through my science book, trying to speed-read the chapter on geological volcanic formations.

Stanley was jogging along beside me, trying to get my attention.

"Don't you want to know what it is?" he asked, panting.

"When the Earth's plates shift, mountains ranges are formed by the upward movement of rock," I read out loud, ignoring Stanley.

"That can wait," insisted Stanley impatiently. "This is important."

"Seismic activity in the upper region of the crust can result in eruptions of dormant volcanic craters," I continued.

Stanley stopped running. "It was a spaceship!" he yelled as I kept going.

I stopped dead in my tracks, still holding the science book open.

"What did you say?" I asked, turning around and looking at Stanley, who was bent over trying to catch his breath.

"A spaceship," he repeated. "The thing that burned the ground. It was a spaceship."

Suddenly I forgot all about my science test. I closed the book and stuffed it into my backpack. Then I walked back to where Stanley was standing.

"Run that one by me again," I said. "How do you know it was a spaceship that did that?"

"It was the pie plate," he said.

Now I was really confused. "What pie plate? What are you talking about? Because if this is some weird dream you had or something, I need to study."

"I figured it out last night," said Stanley. "When I got home from the train—well, from you know where—my mother was baking a pie. Blueberry pie. It smelled great."

"Get to the part about the spaceship," I said.

"Okay, well, when I came home, she was just taking it out of the oven. It was really hot. She hadn't taken out the cooling rack, so she set the pie right on the kitchen counter. When she picked it up again, there was a big scorch mark on the countertop. She was really ticked off."

"I'm still not seeing this," I said.

Stanley sighed. "Don't you get it? The heat that burned the ground came from underneath something, just like my mom setting the hot pie plate on the counter. Something really hot sat on that ground."

"I get it," I said. "And that's why no one called the fire department, because it wasn't a bonfire at all."

"That's my guess," said Stanley. "At first I didn't make the connection. But when I snuck downstairs in the middle of the night to cut a piece of pie, I was picking up the pie plate when it occurred to me that it was shaped just like a flying saucer from one of those old sci-fi movies. That's when I got it."

"You and your stomach," I said. "But it makes sense. The ship's engines would be underneath it, so there wouldn't be any sign of fire. And a big ship could easily scorch the whole area like that."

"Which means that the orange glow we saw *was* a spaceship," said Stanley.

This was our biggest find to date in our hunt for weirdness. A spaceship made everything else look like fun-house attractions.

"Okay," I said, trying to think. "So if an alien ship landed in the train yard, then those tracks we saw must belong . . ."

"To an alien," said Stanley, finishing my sentence. His eyes were wide. "That means we were tracking something from outer space."

The idea that we had been close to a creature from another planet was really cool. But then I remembered something.

"If this really is about aliens, then what does that make the train depot? And the guy in it? Is he an alien?"

"He did ask us which ship we came on," said Stanley, "so he must know something about it. But he didn't look like an alien to me, at least not the kind you see in movies."

My head was swimming with all kinds of ideas. But there was no time to sort them all out. I looked at my watch and saw that we only had five minutes to get to school.

"Come on," I said, sprinting down the sidewalk. "We'll have to talk about this after school. I can't miss this test."

We ran the rest of the way to school and dashed through the doors with only a minute to spare. Stanley went to his class and I went to mine. I slid into my seat just as the bell rang and Mr. Upshaw slapped a test paper in front of me.

"Nice of you to come, Mr. Taylor," he said, grinning. "I thought you were going to miss our little party this morning."

"Not for anything in the world," I said. "Or out of this world, for that matter."

I turned my paper over and looked at the questions. Because I hadn't read the chapter, almost none of it made any sense to me. But it didn't matter anyway. All I could think about was that there might be a spaceship right here in Eerie. It didn't seem possible. Then again, most of the stuff Stanley and I had seen since the weirdness rip opened up wouldn't have seemed possible before.

I tried to answer the test questions as well as I could, but I knew I'd failed. When the bell rang, I took my paper up to Mr. Upshaw's desk and handed it to him. Then I went to my next class, which was English.

Unfortunately, we had a surprise quiz in that class as well, and I did just as badly as I'd done on the science test. In fact, the whole day was one big disaster after another. But I barely noticed, because I was thinking about the spaceship and who or what might have been driving it.

When the final bell of the day rang, I crammed all of my books in my locker and went to meet

Stanley, who was sitting on the front steps of the school. As it turned out, he'd had a bad day as well.

"I got whacked in the head during dodge ball in gym," he said. "I was thinking about the spaceship, and the next thing I knew I was lying on the ground looking up at Coach Withers's face. He wasn't too happy when I screamed, but for a second there I thought I was on an alien examination table."

"I've had aliens on the brain all day, too," I said. "I can't wait to get back out to the train yard and look around some more."

"But we promised Mrs. Crisp that we'd come help her after school," said Stanley.

I groaned. I'd forgotten all about Mrs. Crisp, and even all about Halloween. Suddenly, her costume shop wasn't as exciting as it had been the day before, when there were no spaceships in Eerie.

"Can't we say we have something else we need to do?" I said.

"I don't know," said Stanley. "She's been really nice to us. After all, she gave us those cool costumes. And she sounded so excited about the parade. I think we should help her out."

"You're right," I said. "Besides, I think it's better if we go back to the train depot at night. We don't want anyone seeing us out there."

"It's not who sees us I'm worried about," said Stanley. "It's what *we* might see."

We walked over to the Monster Factory and went inside. Mrs. Crisp was standing at the counter. Sitting beside her was a big stack of papers.

"Oh, I'm so glad you're here," she said when she saw us. "I've been making posters all day."

She held up one of the sheets of paper for us to read:

HALLOWEEN PARADE AND PARTY
Wednesday, October 31
Parade begins at 4:30
Party afterward on the town hall lawn
Prizes, Games, Costume Contest

"What do you think?" asked Mrs. Crisp.

"It looks great," I said. "I really like your drawing of Dracula."

"Actually, that's supposed to be the Mummy," said Mrs. Crisp. "But I couldn't draw his bandages quite right, so I just stuck some fangs on him."

"Well, it looks fine," Stanley said reassuringly. "No one will ever know the difference."

"This is so exciting," said Mrs. Crisp. "This morning I went around to some of the other businesses and told them about the parade. We're each going to make a store float for the parade."

"Float?" I asked.

"Yes," said Mrs. Crisp. "You know, like the ones in the big Thanksgiving Day parade that Mucky's department store holds every year. We're each going to make a Halloween-themed float. Will you two help me with ours?"

The last thing I wanted to do was spend more time away from our alien hunt. But Mrs. Crisp looked so hopeful that I couldn't say no.

"Of course we will," I said. "What do you have in mind?"

"I have a wonderful idea," said Mrs. Crisp. "But first let's go hang all of these posters."

She gave us each a stack of posters and a roll of tape, and the three of us went out onto the street and started hanging them up. By the time I reached the end of the street, my tape was running out.

"Is there any more tape?" I asked Mrs. Crisp.

"Back in the shop," she said. "In the back room. Just go on in and get some. It should be on the workbench."

I left Stanley with Mrs. Crisp and ran back to the store. I went through the curtain that separated the front part of the store from the back, and looked around the workroom. It was really messy. There were costumes everywhere, as well as rows and rows of rubber masks. It was a little creepy, looking at all of those different faces staring down at me, and I wanted just to find the tape and get out again.

I searched the workbench, but I couldn't find any tape. Then I noticed another doorway on one side of the room. Thinking that maybe it was a supply closet, I went over and opened the door.

On the other side wasn't a closet, but a room filled with electronic equipment. All around the room there were machines humming and little colored lights blinking. One machine had a big screen covered in green circles that grew larger and smaller as a bunch of numbers flashed around them. Another machine spit out long pieces of paper covered in some kind of writing. I picked one of the pieces up and looked at it, but I couldn't read it.

I had no idea what any of the equipment was. It all looked very sophisticated, like the kind of stuff a spy would have. But I couldn't figure out why a little old lady who ran a costume store would have it in her back room.

As I was looking around, one of the machines began to hum more loudly than the others, and I went over to look at it. It was a small screen, and it was blank. Then, suddenly, words began to flow across the bottom of the screen.

AGENT 784, ARE YOU THERE?

The words sat there on the screen as I stared at them. Agent 784? Who was that?

Whoever was typing the words seemed to be waiting for an answer. There was a keyboard attached to the screen. I decided to take a chance, and typed in AGENT 784 HERE.

I held my breath as I waited to see what would come next. There was a pause, and then I received a reply: THERE WILL BE ANOTHER ARRIVAL SOON. BE PREPARED TO MEET IT. OPERATION SURPRISE FROM THE SKIES IS BEGINNING.

Arrival? Operation Surprise from the Skies? What was this? I didn't know what to say. Fortunately, the screen went blank again, and I figured whoever was on the other end was gone.

I stared at the screen for a minute longer, but nothing more appeared. I just kept running the message over and over in my head, trying to make sense of it.

Then it came to me, just like Stanley had figured out the pie plate spaceship connection. Mrs. Crisp was some kind of spy, and probably an alien spy. Whoever sent her the message was telling her to meet a spaceship that was arriving. It was all starting to make sense.

Then I had another thought: I'd left Stanley alone with an alien.

5

I had to get Stanley away from Mrs. Crisp. But I couldn't let her know that I had discovered her secret. If she found out I knew, there was no telling what she would do. Besides, we had to find out what she was up to, and how she was connected to the goings-on over at the old train yard.

I ran out of the back room and out the front door. I could see Stanley and Mrs. Crisp at the end of the block, still hanging up posters. I tried to compose myself as I walked back toward them. I didn't want her to suspect anything was up.

"Hi," I said, trying to sound as casual as possible.

"There you are," said Mrs. Crisp. "We were starting to think that something had happened to you."

"No," I said. "I was just—um—looking for the tape."

"Wasn't it on the workbench?" asked Mrs. Crisp.

"I couldn't find it," I said. "You must have hidden it—I mean, put it somewhere else."

"Are you okay, Mitchell?" asked Stanley. "You look a little flushed."

"Couldn't be better," I said, and tried to laugh. But it came out as more of a snort.

"Well, it doesn't matter about the tape," said Mrs. Crisp. "We've used up all the posters anyway. Now we have to think about the party."

"Oh, I almost forgot," I said quickly. "Stanley and I have to get to the library before it closes."

"We do?" asked Stanley. "Why?"

"We have to look up that information," I said, raising my eyebrows to let him know something was up. "You know, for the project."

"Sure," said Stanley, getting my meaning. "Right. That. Yeah, we have to get to the library."

"That's fine," said Mrs. Crisp. "I'll just make up a list of what we need. But perhaps you can come back tomorrow and help me with the float. I told you, I have a great idea for it."

"We'll come back," I said, taking Stanley's arm and practically dragging him away. "Tomorrow."

We had turned and started to walk down the sidewalk when Mrs. Crisp came running after us.

"Just a moment," she called, and we stopped. I was sure she knew I'd found out about her. My heart started to beat wildly as I waited for her to pull out a ray gun or some other alien weapon and blast us to bits. When she reached into her purse, I let out a gasp. But all she did was pull out a flyer for the parade.

"Would you be a couple of dears and put this up in the library?" she asked.

I let out a sigh of relief as I took the flyer from her. "Sure," I said. "No problem."

She smiled, and we went on our way. As soon as we were out of her sight, Stanley turned to me.

"Okay, what is going on?"

I told Stanley all about what I'd seen in the back room of the Monster Factory.

"It was so weird," I said. "I wish you could have seen it."

"So do I," said Stanley. "Do you really think Mrs. Crisp is an alien? She seems so nice."

"What else could she be?" I asked. "I think the message on the computer screen says it all. And look at how she just suddenly appeared here. I bet she's on some kind of a mission."

"So what do we do about her?" asked Stanley. "We can't just ask her if she's an alien. And why would an alien want to come to Eerie and have a Halloween parade?"

"That's what we have to find out," I said. "And I think we should start by going back to the train yard tonight."

We did go by the library and hang up the poster, just in case Mrs. Crisp was following us. We even spent some time looking at the card catalog and pretending to check out some books. Then we left and went back to the Secret Spot to plan our next move.

"The machines in the Monster Factory looked pretty high tech," I said, once we'd locked the door and pulled the blinds down. "We're going to have to be really careful. Who knows what kind of alien technology she's got up her sleeve?"

"If they can make that depot look like a wreck on the outside while the inside is in perfect condition, then they have some pretty powerful stuff," agreed Stanley.

"That must be their base of operations," I said. "I bet all of their big secrets are hidden in there."

"Which means they'll do anything to keep us from finding them," said Stanley. "How are we going to do this?"

"Carefully," I said. "And we'll start by making sure we're prepared for tonight."

For the next hour we pulled together our spy

kits, making sure our backpacks held everything we might need. I also found some black clothes to wear, so that it would be harder to see us in the dark.

The hardest part was sitting through dinner. I wanted to get going, but we had to wait until it was dark. We also didn't want to make our parents think anything strange was going on. So I sat there picking at my lasagna while my father went on and on about his radio show.

"It's going to be so great," he said. "I've got some guys coming in to do sound effects while we perform. So when the aliens land, there will actually be the sound of a spaceship door opening. You'll even hear their lasers when they fire at people."

"That sounds great, Dad," said Kari. "I bet everyone will be scared silly."

"What are your big Halloween plans, Mitchell?" my mother asked.

I pushed a piece of lasagna around with my fork. If she'd asked me that question the day before, I would have told her all about the parade and how Stanley and I were helping Mrs. Crisp plan it. Now Mrs. Crisp was an alien enemy, and Stanley and I were the only ones who knew about it.

"I don't know," I answered. "Probably the usual."

"Do you have your costumes picked out yet?" my father asked.

The costumes. I hadn't even thought about them. No wonder they were so realistic. I bet Mrs. Crisp had seen a lot of alien bounty hunters up close, and probably even a Karakian moon guppy. She might even *be* a Karakian moon guppy for all I knew.

"We're not sure what we want to be yet," I said.

My dad went back to talking about *War of the Worlds,* and I tried to eat some of my lasagna. When I figured that I'd pushed it around long enough, I asked to be excused and took my plate into the kitchen. Then I went upstairs, changed into my black clothes, and went downstairs again. I ducked out before anyone could see me and ask any questions.

Stanley was waiting for me by the garage, and he also had on his black outfit. We looked like a couple of cat burglars as we got on our bikes and rode for the train yard.

The moon was brighter than it had been the night before, so we tried to stay in the shadows as we made our way back to the yard. This time we left our bikes at the top of the hill overlooking the trains and walked down because we didn't want to give ourselves away.

First we went back and looked at the circle of tracks. The soot on the ground was gone, and all traces of the footprints were swept away.

"They cleaned house," I said as we surveyed the litter-strewn ground. "They know we're on to them."

"I bet they've set a trap for us, too," added Stanley. "Watch your step."

Since the aliens had cleaned up after themselves, I had a feeling that they had probably locked the door to the depot as well. Sure enough, when we went back to the Eerie Cola poster and tried to go through, all we felt under our fingers was paper, and underneath that, scratchy brick.

"Great," said Stanley. "A dead end. I guess we should have known. Now we'll never figure out what's going on."

"Don't be so sure about that," a voice whispered behind us.

Stanley and I both just about jumped out of our skins when we wheeled around to see who was talking to us. I expected to be standing face-to-face with a death-ray-wielding alien with four heads and purple teeth. But the person standing there was anything but unusual looking.

The man was perfectly ordinary. He was wearing a greasy mechanic's uniform that had the name BUD stitched over the shirt pocket, and he looked like any guy who worked at any gas station in the country. In fact, he was the guy who worked at the gas station on Main Street. He'd filled up my mom's car a lot of times, but until now he had never spoken a word to me.

"Sorry about that," he said, smiling. "Didn't mean to scare you."

"That's okay," I replied. "What are you doing here?"

"I might ask you the same question," he said. "But I think I know the answer. You're looking for the spacemen."

"What spacemen?" asked Stanley innocently.

"Good try," said Bud. "Playing like you don't know. Look, you don't have to worry. I'm on your side. In fact, that's why I'm here. We need your help."

"Our help?" I said.

Bud nodded. "I know you think I'm just the guy from the gas station," he said. "But it's just a disguise. I work for an organization that keeps an eye on things like this."

"Things like what?" asked Stanley.

"Aliens," said Bud. "We track 'em. And what we have inside this building here is one big hive of aliens just waiting to break out."

I looked at Stanley. I didn't know whether we could trust Bud or not, but right at that moment we didn't really have much choice.

"Tell you what," said Bud. "I'll take you inside and show you just what's going on."

"You can get in?" I asked.

"We've learned a thing or two about their technology," Bud said.

He reached into his shirt pocket and took out what looked like two small pins. He came over and attached them to our shirts.

"These are cloaking devices," he said. "They make you look like aliens. That way we can walk around without being noticed."

"Wow," I said. "You guys have learned a lot. Do these things really work?"

"Let's go find out," Bud said. "I found their new door earlier."

He walked around to the back of the train depot. More posters covered the wall there. He walked up to one that had a picture of a man petting a big, fluffy collie dog and stepped right through it. Stanley and I followed behind him, and slipped through the hidden door as easily as if we were walking into our own houses.

We were back inside the train station. Only this time, instead of being empty, the place was filled. But it wasn't people who were walking around the place—it was aliens. All kinds of aliens.

All Stanley and I could do was stand there with our mouths open as we looked at the different creatures passing by us. Some of them were tall and covered in blue fur. Others were the size of monkeys, only they had huge heads and seven eyes. Still others looked almost exactly like humans, only with long tails that whipped around as they walked.

"What are they?" I asked Bud.

"Oh, these are your standard Level One aliens," he said. "Venusians, Uranians, a few Martians. Nothing too serious yet."

"What are they doing here?" Stanley asked.

"Visiting," said Bud.

"Visiting?" I said. "Visiting who?"

"Earth," said Bud. "See, this place is a sort of airport for alien spaceships. They stop here and let aliens off. Then the aliens go to different parts of the Earth."

"An alien airport?" I asked. "Why here in Eerie?"

"We don't exactly know," said Bud. "It just opened up a little while ago. We aren't sure why they picked this particular place."

"I wonder if it has to do with that thing you saw, Mitch," said Stanley. "What was it called—

Operation Surprise from the Skies or something?"

"What!" said Bud, startled. "You know about Operation Surprise from the Skies?"

"Yeah," I answered. "I saw something about it at the Monster Factory."

Bud looked worried. "Then things are proceeding more quickly than we expected."

"What things?" I asked, trying not to stare at a two-headed green creature that was ambling by.

"There are some things I need to explain to you," said Bud. "But not here. It isn't safe. Although they see us as aliens just like themselves, the cloaking devices can't always hide our language differences. Let's go somewhere else."

We followed Bud as he walked through the crowded train station, pushing past the aliens until he reached a stairway. He went up the stairs, and we climbed up right behind him. At the top, he pushed open a door and went into a small room.

"This is better," he said after he'd shut the door. "No one will bother us here."

"You sure know your way around," said Stanley.

"I've been making a lot of visits here," said Bud. "Ever since we found it."

"So who exactly is this 'we' you keep talking

about?" I asked him. "And what does Mrs. Crisp have to do with all of this?"

Bud sat down on a chair, and motioned for us to sit as well. "Something big is happening in Eerie," he said when we were seated. "Something very big. From what we've discovered, the aliens are planning on taking over the world, and they're starting right here in Eerie."

"Come on," said Stanley. "That sounds like something out of a science fiction movie. That doesn't really happen."

"Really?" asked Bud. "Is what you've seen out there real? Is it actually happening?"

Stanley swallowed. "I guess so," he admitted.

"I know it's a lot to take in all at once," said Bud gently. "But you have to try. The aliens are using Eerie as a starting point for taking over the world. We don't know exactly how or when, but we know they're planning it. And Mrs. Crisp is leading the way."

"I knew it!" I said. "I knew she was the ringleader. What is she, a Martian?"

"We're not sure," said Bud. "But we do know she's the one to watch. I've been keeping an eye on her from the gas station. That's my disguise."

"Good one," said Stanley. "I would never have guessed you were an alien hunter."

"Thanks," said Bud. "Anyway, I've been watching Mrs. Crisp. That's how I knew that you two could be trusted. She wouldn't have taken an interest in you if she didn't think she had to keep an eye on you."

"What's she afraid of?" I asked. "We're just a couple of kids."

"Who knows?" said Bud. "But as long as she's interested in you, that means you can help us."

"Help you do what?" I asked.

Bud looked at Stanley, then at me. "We need you to help us save the world."

6

"Come on," I said. "That saving-the-world stuff is just in movies. Things like that don't really happen to real kids."

Bud shook his head. "This is real," he insisted. "From what we've seen, the aliens have developed technology that will make it almost impossible to stop them. That's why we've got to try and figure out what Mrs. Crisp is up to. It's our only chance at fighting them."

"Well, she is planning a Halloween parade," said Stanley. "But I don't see how that's a big threat to civilization or anything."

Bud thought for a minute. "It could be a diversion," he said. "Maybe she wants everyone to be at the parade so that something else can happen without anyone knowing it."

"You mean, like Operation Surprise from the Skies?" I suggested.

"It would be a brilliant move," said Bud. "Just the sort of thing a sneaky one like her would do. While everyone is at the parade, the aliens sneak in and take over. Very clever."

"So then, let's make sure the parade never happens," said Stanley.

"No," said Bud. "We want it to go on. We don't want her to think that anyone is suspicious of her. And the two of you are going to help her."

"What?" I exclaimed. "You want us to help the aliens? Are you nuts?"

"I know it sounds strange," said Bud. "But we need them to think that their plan is working. Otherwise, who knows what they'll do? You saw that bunch down in the depot. Do you want them running all over Eerie?"

I shook my head. "Not on your life," I said.

"Me, neither," agreed Stanley. "But I don't know if I can work with her, knowing that she's really from outer space."

"I wonder what she looks like under that disguise," I said.

"Trust me," said Bud. "You probably don't want to know. But it's very important that the two of you act as though everything is perfectly normal. Do whatever she says. Don't let on that anything even remotely weird is going on. But if you can, try to get another look at that back room of hers.

It would really help if we could find out exactly how much she knows about Operation Surprise from the Skies."

I took a deep breath. "Okay," I said. "We can do this."

I turned to Stanley. "We just have to stick together and remember that the safety of Eerie and the Earth is at stake."

Stanley looked at Bud. "How can you do this all the time?" he asked. "You know, walk around with all those aliens? It would really creep me out."

Bud laughed. "You get used to it," he said. "Sometimes I even forget what humans look like. Then I go back to the real world and think the people around me look weird."

"Well, I would never get used to it," Stanley said.

"If we're lucky, none of us will have to," said Bud. "Now, are you guys ready to go back through that crowd?"

"We're ready," I said. "Let's go."

The three of us left the little room and went back down the stairs. When we stepped into the train depot, we were once again surrounded by aliens. By this time I was a little bit used to the way they looked, but it was still hard not to stare as we walked through them toward the revolving door.

As we neared the exit, the man who looked like a train conductor stepped in front of us. Stanley and I froze in terror, thinking that he'd recognized us from the night before. I was so petrified that I forgot we were being cloaked by the alien devices on our shirts.

"Do you have your tickets?" he demanded.

I almost ran, thinking that we'd been caught. But Bud reached into his pocket and pulled out three pieces of paper.

"Here you go," he said, handing them to the conductor.

The man looked at them, then took a ticket punch out of his pocket and punched them. "Ship for Milwaukee leaves from track twelve in ten minutes," he said. "Have a nice trip."

"Thanks," said Bud.

The man walked away, and we slipped through the door and back into the train yard.

"How come he looks like a human?" I asked after Bud took our cloaking pins off.

"Oh, he just likes the way being human looks," Bud explained. "He's been here a long time. He's actually a giant yellow Plutonian marsh slug."

We walked to the edge of the train yard, where Bud stopped.

"You two go on home now," he said. "I have some more work to do here. And you should probably stay clear of this place from now on. It isn't exactly a safe place to be. If you need to get information to me, just stop by the gas station. But make sure no one sees you doing it. We don't want to blow our cover."

"Right," I said, nodding. "We'll get as much information about Mrs. Crisp and what she's doing as we can."

Bud put his hand on my shoulder. "I'm glad we can count on the two of you," he said. "You have no idea what you're doing for your town, your country, and your planet."

He turned around and walked back into the night, and Stanley and I walked back up the steep hill to our bikes. When we reached the top, we turned and looked down at the crumbling old train depot.

"It's hard to believe that inside it's crawling with aliens, isn't it?" said Stanley. "Makes you wonder what else is hiding around here."

"It's a good thing we ran into Bud," I said. "Otherwise we might have played right into the aliens' hands. Well, Mrs. Crisp isn't going to make fools of us now that we're on to her."

We rode our bikes back home, leaving the train yard, Bud, and the aliens behind. I still couldn't quite believe that we had been walking around in the middle of a bunch of creatures from outer space, or that we were now involved in a plan to save the Earth. I still felt like any kid riding his bike home with his best friend.

But I wasn't just any kid, and neither was Stanley. We were the defenders of the world. After we put the bikes back we stood outside our houses, just sort of looking up at the sky. We didn't say anything, but I knew that, like me, Stanley was thinking about aliens coming to Earth and taking over.

"Don't worry," I said, breaking the silence. "We'll win. I personally don't want to live next door to a big yellow Plutonian marsh slug."

The next day went by quickly, mainly because I got back all of the tests I'd done so badly on the day before, and couldn't wait to forget them. After listening to Mr. Upshaw lecture us on how we were never going to get anywhere in life if we didn't understand the principles of volcanic activity, and to Miss Crandall talk about how *Romeo and Juliet* was the greatest play in the world because it was so sad, I was more than ready to get over to the Monster Factory. After a day of school, even helping out an alien was a welcome relief. In fact, after half an hour of Mr.

Upshaw's lecture, I almost started wishing that aliens *would* take over, just so I wouldn't have to listen to him talk anymore.

Before we entered the Monster Factory I stopped Stanley on the street.

"Remember," I told him, "we have to act like everything is totally fine. She can't know that we know what she is."

"Well, *I'm* certainly not going to tell her," Stanley said.

We opened the door to the shop and went in. Mrs. Crisp wasn't there, so I called out, "Hello?"

A few seconds later, Mrs. Crisp came out from the back room. She was fixing her hair, and seemed a little flustered.

"Sorry I wasn't here," she said as she tucked some stray hairs back into her bun. "I had to—um—answer a very important phone call."

I snuck a sideways look at Stanley. I suspected Mrs. Crisp had been getting another interplanetary message from her alien bosses or planning some evil escapade she didn't want us to know about. Well, I wasn't going to let on that we knew anything.

"That's okay," I said cheerfully. "I'm sure you have a lot of work to do, getting ready for the invasion and all."

"He means for the *parade*," said Stanley

quickly, and I realized that I'd slipped up without meaning to.

"Oh, yeah," I said, trying to cover for myself. "Duh. How stupid of me."

Mrs. Crisp looked at me for what seemed longer than usual, but she didn't say anything except, "Yes, there is a lot to do. For the parade, that is."

"What can we do?" I asked, trying to change the subject.

"Well," said Mrs. Crisp. "I've been getting lots of phone calls from people interested in the parade. Several businesses are going to make floats. Even Bud from the gas station said he'd be making one."

At the mention of Bud, Stanley and I both started to fidget a little bit. I wondered what Mrs. Crisp would think of him if she knew he was out to stop her from conquering the world.

"Really?" I asked. "What kind of float?"

"I don't know," said Mrs. Crisp. "It's a surprise. But I know that our float will be even better."

"What is our float?" asked Stanley.

Mrs. Crisp smiled. "A trick-or-treat bag," she said triumphantly. "We're going to make a big bag out of newspapers and paste. Then, when we pull it along the parade route, someone will stand inside of it and toss out candy to the crowd. It will look like the bag is spouting Halloween candy!"

"What a great idea," I said. It *was* a good idea, and for a moment I forgot that Mrs. Crisp was really a purple three-toed lizard from Alpha Centauri, or maybe a pink-furred giant hamster from the Beta Quadrant.

"Come with me," said Mrs. Crisp, heading for the rear of the store. "I have all of the supplies back here."

We went into the workshop. Mrs. Crisp had cleared a large area, and there were piles of newspapers, rolls of wire, and big buckets. I noticed that the door to what was supposed to be the supply closet was shut.

"This should be everything you need to make the float," she said. "If you can make a bag shape out of the wire, then I'll come back and show you how to put the newspaper on."

She left us alone, and Stanley and I unrolled the wire and bent it into a rough bag shape. It wasn't very difficult, actually, and once we'd tied the wire together, it looked pretty good. The bag was tall enough for someone to stand in without being seen, but not so big that it would be hard to transport.

"Not bad," said Stanley, stepping back to survey our handiwork. "Very—um—baggy."

"I wish I could get a look inside the back room," I said. "I bet there's all kinds of good stuff in there that Bud would like to know about."

"Why don't you go take a look?" suggested Stanley. He walked over to the curtain separating the front of the store from the workroom and looked out. "She's with a couple of customers. I bet she'll be a while. You can look and I'll stand guard. If she starts to come back here, I'll call you."

"Good idea," I said. "But make sure you watch for her. I don't want her catching me in there. If she does, then this is all over."

"Don't worry," said Stanley. "I'll be watching her like a hawk. At the first sign of anything, I'll let you know."

I nodded and went over to the door. It was shut, but it wasn't locked, and all I had to do was pull it open. I gave Stanley a thumbs-up sign and slipped inside.

The room looked exactly the same as it had the first time I'd seen it, although now more of the machines were on and running. I still couldn't make out what most of them were, but that didn't really matter now. All I really needed to do was find some kind of information, some kind of proof that Mrs. Crisp was really involved in an alien plot to invade Eerie.

I knew I didn't have a lot of time, so I started to search for something I could take back to Bud. Unfortunately, there wasn't much of anything. Most of the machines were blinking and buzzing, and their screens were filled with all kinds of information, but none of it meant anything to me. And there was no way I could take an entire machine out of the Monster Factory without Mrs. Crisp noticing.

Just as I was about to give up, I noticed something lying next to one of the machines. It was an ordinary folder—the kind my dad uses to put his notes for classes in. I picked it up and looked at it. Across the front was written OPERATION SURPRISE FROM THE SKIES/TOP SECRET.

I opened the folder and looked at the papers inside. Many of them were covered in a strange kind of writing that I couldn't read at all. But one was in English, and its message was very clear. I took it out and read it.

Operation Surprise from the Skies will commence on Wednesday, October 31, with an initial landing of thirteen ships at Earthbase 01. These ships will carry intelligence officers and soldiers trained in infiltration and capture of human life forms. Once the area of Eerie, Indiana, has been contained and its special properties mined for later use, the second wave will begin, and domination of the world known as Earth will be a quick and easy matter.

I read the paper twice to make sure I wasn't seeing things. If what I was reading was true, then things were a lot more serious than we'd thought. I had to get the information to Bud.

I folded the paper up and stuffed it into my pocket. I put the folder back where I'd found it and turned to leave. But as I was about to go out the door, I saw Stanley turn and wave frantically at me. Mrs. Crisp was coming.

There wasn't enough time for me to leave the secret room before she walked into the workroom. All I could do was pull the door closed and peer out through the crack to see what was happening. I watched as Mrs. Crisp surveyed the work we'd done on the float.

"This is wonderful, Stanley," she said happily. "You and Mitchell have done a fantastic job."

She looked around the room. "Where is Mitchell?" she asked. "Wasn't he in here with you?"

"He was," said Stanley. "But he—um—had to run out."

"Run out?" said Mrs. Crisp.

"Yeah," said Stanley. "He had to go get some more wire for the float."

"But there's lots of wire left," said Mrs. Crisp, picking up a bunch that was on the floor.

"Oh," said Stanley. "Well, it's—um—not the right kind. He wanted some special wire."

Mrs. Crisp looked confused. "I didn't see him leave," she said. "That's peculiar."

"I think you were helping some customers," said Stanley. "You probably just missed him."

"Probably," said Mrs. Crisp, but she didn't sound convinced. "Well, you might as well get started on covering this with the newspaper and paste. I'll just go get the paste. It's in the closet over there."

She started to walk toward the secret room. If she opened the door, she'd definitely find me. There was nowhere I could possibly hide. And if that happened, everything would be over. All I could do was stand there watching helplessly as she got closer and closer.

By the look on Stanley's face, I could tell that he was as terrified as I was. He just stood by the float, his eyes wide as Mrs. Crisp reached for the door.

But as she was pulling the door open, the bell over the front door rang. Or rather, screamed.

"Oh, that must be a customer," said Mrs. Crisp,

letting go of the doorknob. "I'll just go see who it is. Then we can get started."

She left the workroom. As soon as she was gone, I dashed out of the back room and shut the door behind me.

"That was close," said Stanley. "I thought you were a goner for sure."

"You and me both," I said. "Another second and we would have been alien lunch."

"What did you find?" asked Stanley.

I couldn't answer his question, because just then Mrs. Crisp returned.

"It was just someone looking for some plastic fangs for a vampire costume," she said as she walked in. When she saw me, she looked surprised. "Mitchell," she said. "I thought you were gone."

"I came back," I said uneasily. I hoped she wouldn't ask any more questions, because I was so nervous I would definitely blow it. "I—uh—didn't find the wire."

"That's okay," said Mrs. Crisp after looking at me for a moment. "I think the float looks wonderful. Are you boys ready for the fun part now?"

"You bet," said Stanley. "We can't wait to get started."

"I'll just get the paste," said Mrs. Crisp, and headed for the door to the secret room again. But when she reached it, she stopped. "That's odd," she said. "I know I shut this door when I left."

Mrs. Crisp turned and glared at us. She didn't look happy. "You two weren't poking around in there, were you?" she asked menacingly.

Suddenly, the paper in my pocket felt like it was on fire. I was sure it would burn a hole right through my jeans and fall onto the floor where Mrs. Crisp would see it and know what we were up to. I wracked my brain, hoping some kind of answer would come to me. But nothing would. All I could do was stand there looking at Mrs. Crisp's face and thinking about what she might be planning on doing to us if she found out I'd been inside her secret room.

Then I felt my mouth opening, and before I knew it I was saying the only thing my brain could process. "Run!" I yelled at Stanley as I turned and bolted for the front of the store. "Run for your life!"

7

I ran as fast as I could, and Stanley was right behind me. As I pushed open the front door, I heard Mrs. Crisp calling to us.

"Wait!" she shouted. "Come back here!"

Part of me wanted to stop, but a bigger part of me didn't, and that part won the argument. I tore out of the Monster Factory as though Dracula himself were chasing me, and took off down the block. I heard Stanley's sneakers pounding on the sidewalk behind me, and as we ran past store after store, Mrs. Crisp's voice grew more and more faint, until finally I couldn't hear her at all.

I turned the corner by World of Stuff and stopped. Leaning against the wall, I tried to catch my breath and calm down. Stanley slumped to the ground next to me, panting. After a few minutes my wildly beating heart stopped thumping quite so much, and I was able to talk again.

"Do you think she suspects anything?" I asked hopefully.

Stanley groaned. "Oh, no," he said. "I'm sure she thinks we just ran out of there screaming because we're afraid of paste."

"You don't have to be sarcastic," I shot back. "I didn't see you coming up with any brilliant ideas."

"What were you so spooked about, anyway?" asked Stanley. "Did you find a giant alien egg in there or something?"

"Let's go inside," I said, nodding at the door of World of Stuff. "I don't think she'll try to get us in broad daylight."

We went inside and took two seats at the soda counter.

"Hello there, boys," said Mr. Crawford. "Can I get you the usual?"

"Sure, Mr. Crawford," I said. "Two Black Cows, heavy on the black."

"Must be a rough afternoon," he said, smiling, as he poured root beer and chocolate into two glasses and added vanilla ice cream.

"You don't know the half of it," I said.

Mr. Crawford put our drinks in front of us and then went off to rearrange the yo-yo display. As soon as he was out of earshot I pulled the paper

I'd snagged from Mrs. Crisp's secret lair out of my pocket and unfolded it.

"Take a look at this," I told Stanley as I smoothed out the paper and laid it on the counter.

Stanley took a long sip of his Black Cow before he picked up the paper and read it over. Then he took another long sip before he finally said, "We're in trouble."

"We were already in trouble." I sighed. "Now we're in *big* trouble. I don't know *what* we're going to do now."

"I guess we should go tell Bud," said Stanley, taking a slurp that drained half his glass.

"He's going to be really mad," I said, putting my head in my hands. "We really blew it. *I* really blew it."

"Look," said Stanley. "It's not like we're pros at this secret-agent stuff, all right? We're going to make mistakes once in a while."

"This isn't just a mistake," I said, getting hysterical. "This is aliens taking over the world, and we were supposed to stop it. But instead, I pretty much told the head alien that we're on to her, or it, or whatever it is. Now, because of me, Eerie is going to be the number one vacation spot for seven-eyed tree frogs from Neptune. So I don't know how you can just sit there sucking down a Black Cow and not freaking out."

Stanley sighed. "What do you want me to do?" he asked. "I *am* freaked out, okay? But that's not going to change anything. The aliens aren't going to care if I freak out or not, so right now I'm just going to sit here and enjoy what might possibly be my very last Black Cow as a resident of alien-free Earth."

For a minute I was really mad at Stanley. He seemed so calm just sitting there, sipping through his straw and ignoring completely the piece of alien evidence still sitting on the counter by his elbow. I couldn't understand why he wasn't scared like I was.

Then I realized that he was right. There wasn't anything we could do to change what was happening. At least not yet. I also knew that he was as scared as I was, probably even more scared. But he knew that running around shrieking about it wasn't going to help. When I looked at it that way, it made perfect sense to sit in World of Stuff watching Mr. Crawford putting the yo-yos in order and drinking my drink. So that's what I did.

Stanley and I sat there in silence for about ten minutes, neither of us saying a word as we finished our Black Cows. When we were done, we paid Mr. Crawford and left. Then we walked over to the gas station, taking the back way in case Mrs. Crisp was prowling around looking for us. But we didn't see any sign of her as we snuck up to the rear of the station and looked through the window.

Bud was sitting in the office, his feet propped up on the desk while he read the newspaper and drank a soda. When I tapped on the window to get his attention, he nearly fell backward in his chair from surprise. When he righted himself and turned around, he squinted at our faces through the grimy window for a few seconds before recognizing us. Then he waved for us to meet him at the back door.

Stanley and I went inside the garage. I made sure the door was closed before I said anything.

"She knows about us," I said. "I mean, she knows that we know about her."

"Crisp?" asked Bud, as though there were fifteen alien spies running around and he couldn't remember which one we were supposed to be watching.

"Is there another one?" asked Stanley, as if he'd read my mind.

"Oh—um—no, not that I know of," said Bud. He was a little distracted, and it seemed to me that he wasn't taking our news very seriously.

"So now what do we do?" I asked.

Bud didn't say anything. He seemed to be looking at the floor.

"Bud?" I prompted, and then when he didn't answer, "Bud!"

"What?" Bud exclaimed. "Oh. Well, let me see here."

"You don't seem too concerned about this," said Stanley. "Did we or did we not just expose your entire operation?"

"I suppose so," said Bud. "I mean, you did if she knows you're here. Does she know?"

"Of course not," I said. "I may be stupid, but I'm not *that* stupid."

"Okay then," said Bud, sounding much more confident. "In that case, the solution to our problem is easy."

"And what would that be?" I asked when Bud didn't continue.

"Oh," said Bud again. He seemed to be thinking about anything but the Mrs. Crisp situation. "We—um—we capture her. Take her out of the picture. That way she can't tell her alien friends what's going on."

"Won't they just assume she's been captured and get angry?" asked Stanley.

"Maybe," said Bud. "But they won't know what

to do about it. So that's what we do—we trap her."

"And just how do we do that?" I asked. "We can't just walk up to her and grab her. You said those aliens have all kinds of weapons."

"They do," answered Bud. "They do. But I'm sure you'll come up with something."

"Us?" asked Stanley and I together. "Why do we have to do it?"

"Do I have to do everything?" replied Bud angrily. "Okay, here's what we'll do. You lure her somewhere. Tell her you have information she wants. When she gets there, we'll trap her."

"Good plan," I said. "So where should we tell her to meet us?"

"How about the train depot?" suggested Stanley.

"No!" said Bud. "Anywhere but there!"

I looked at Bud. He was sweating, and looked really frightened—like just mentioning the train depot had terrified him.

"What's wrong?" I asked him.

Bud pulled out a handkerchief and wiped his forehead with it. "Well, it's just that the depot is the center of alien activity," he said. "She would be able to call for help. It would be better to meet her someplace far away from there."

"Okay," I said. "How about the cemetery?

That's deserted, and it's far away from the depot."

"Fine," said Bud. "That's just fine. You set it up for tonight. I'll meet you there at nine."

Bud showed us to the door and we left. Once again staying away from the main streets, we headed toward home.

"Bud sure was acting weird," said Stanley. "What do you think was wrong with him?"

"Just nervous, I guess," I said. "He's probably afraid he'll get into trouble with the people he works for or something."

"Do you really think we'll be able to get Mrs. Crisp to come to the graveyard tonight?"

I nodded. "She'll come," I said. "You know how those aliens are. They're always ready for a showdown."

"Since when are you an expert on aliens?" asked Stanley.

"Since one started trying to take over my town," I replied. "Besides, I've seen a lot of movies. The aliens always fall for the old meet-us-in-the-cemetery trick."

We reached my house without running into Mrs. Crisp, and went upstairs to the Secret Spot. Picking up the phone, I dialed the Monster Factory. As the phone rang, I drummed my fingers nervously on the desk. When the phone rang for the seventh time without anyone picking up, I was about to hang up. Then I heard the click of someone answering.

"Hello," said Mrs. Crisp's voice. "The Monster Factory."

"Hi," I said stupidly. "This is Mitchell."

"Mitchell," said Mrs. Crisp eagerly. "I'm so glad it's you. I want to talk to you about this afternoon."

Mrs. Crisp sounded so happy to be talking to me that I almost forgot why I'd called her. But then I remembered, and I became very business-like.

"Look," I said. "I don't have time for chitchat. We know about Operation Surprise from the Skies."

"You do?" asked Mrs. Crisp slowly. "What do you know about it?"

"That doesn't matter now," I said, trying my best to sound like I knew what I was doing. "What matters is that we're on to you. We should meet and discuss this."

"Well, then," said Mrs. Crisp. "Where did you have in mind?"

"The cemetery," I said. "Tonight at nine o'clock."

"Mitchell," said Mrs. Crisp. "There's really no need for this. Can't we just—"

"No," I snapped, cutting her off. "Tonight at the cemetery. Be there."

I hung up, feeling very proud of myself.

"You were great!" said Stanley. "You really let that old alien know who's boss."

"Thanks," I said. "I hope it works."

For the next couple of hours we paced around the Secret Spot, planning how we would act that night at the cemetery. Stanley thought we should tell someone else where we were going, just in case something went wrong, but I vetoed that idea.

"We'd have to tell them why we were going to the cemetery," I said. "And you know they'd never go for that."

In the end, we told our parents that we were going over to the library to work on book reports. My father was so busy telling us about the rehearsals for his *War of the Worlds* program that no one really noticed anyway. Stanley's mom and dad were going out bowling, and they wouldn't be home until late. So we managed to get out of our houses without any fuss at all.

"I'm glad this turned out to be so easy," said Stanley as we rode our bikes toward the cemetery, "but it seems like saving the world should be a little bit more exciting, doesn't it?"

"I know what you mean," I said. "Chasing a

little old woman around isn't quite as exciting as having a shoot-out in space. But I think we have to work up to that stuff. You know—start small. This will be good practice."

When we reached the cemetery, we still had half an hour before it was nine o'clock. I looked around for Bud, but he was nowhere in sight. Then I realized that we hadn't told Mrs. Crisp exactly where in the cemetery to meet us.

"She could be anywhere," I said. "We'll have to go look for her. And we'll have to find Bud at the same time."

We left the bikes at the entrance to the cemetery and started walking. We'd brought our flashlights, but didn't want to turn them on, in case Mrs. Crisp had brought some friends along. That meant that we had to make our way through the tombstones slowly, trying not to trip over anything or fall into any open holes. I tried to forget that they were graves.

The Eerie cemetery isn't the most cheerful place, even on a sunny day, and on a cold October night right before Halloween when you're going to meet an alien who doesn't exactly like you, it can be downright creepy. The trees had abandoned most of their leaves, and their bare skeletons stuck up from the ground like bony hands trying to grab at the moon, which was almost full. Besides, the shadows thrown by the towering gravestones made it hard to know what was real and what was just a piece of darkness.

We had just walked up a small rise when I saw a light bobbing around ahead of us. I grabbed Stanley's arm and pointed to the light, which was moving up and down as someone walked among the graves.

"Look," I hissed. "Someone is here already."

"But is it Bud or Mrs. Crisp?" asked Stanley. "I can't tell in the dark."

"It's Mrs. Crisp," said a voice behind us, making us both jump about two feet in the air. I almost screamed. It was Bud.

"You have got to stop doing that," I scolded. "One of these days you're going to give me a heart attack."

"Sorry," said Bud.

"How did you get in here so quickly?" asked Stanley. "And how did you know where we were?"

"I see well in the dark," said Bud. "That's how I know that's Crisp up there."

"So we're here and she's here," I said. "So now what?" It suddenly dawned on me that we had absolutely no plan at all.

"You two get her over here," said Bud. "I'll take care of the rest."

Bud crept behind a big gravestone that was

carved into the shape of a heart with an angel sitting on top of it. When he was completely hidden, I turned and called out to Mrs. Crisp.

"Hey!" I shouted. "We're over here."

The light turned and started coming toward us as Mrs. Crisp picked her way through the graveyard. When she was about twenty feet away, I held up my hand.

"That's far enough," I said. "Don't come any closer."

Mrs. Crisp was dressed in a heavy wool coat and was wearing a knit hat. She looked like any old lady out for a walk at night. Looking at her standing there, I felt like I was talking to my grandma.

"Mitchell," said Mrs. Crisp. "There's a perfectly good explanation for all of this. If you'd just listen—"

"No," I said. "We know your tricks. Now you just do as I say."

I fished in the pocket of my pants and held up the piece of paper I'd taken from her secret room. "We know all about Operation Surprise from the Skies," I yelled. "We know what you're up to!"

"But you don't understand," Mrs. Crisp said. "I'm not . . ."

As she spoke, she reached for something inside her coat.

"She's got a laser!" I shouted, and dropped to the ground.

From somewhere in the darkness, Bud jumped up and ran at Mrs. Crisp. I heard her gasp as he grabbed her, and then the two of them were thrashing around in the leaves.

When I stood up, Bud was holding Mrs. Crisp by the arm. He had wrapped a cloth around her mouth so that she couldn't speak, and her hands were tied behind her back.

"I got her," he said triumphantly. "She put up a good fight, but I got her."

Mrs. Crisp was trying to say something through her gag, but all she could do was gurgle and moan. I was glad I couldn't hear what she was saying, because I was sure it was something unpleasant.

"Turn off her cloaking device," said Stanley. "Let's see what she really is."

"That's not a good idea," said Bud. "It might—um—give her some kind of an advantage or something. I'm going to take her somewhere for safekeeping. I want the two of you to go home now. Tomorrow we'll meet and talk about what to do next. You've been a big help to us. We won't forget it."

Bud started to walk Mrs. Crisp through the cemetery and away from the front gate. I didn't know where he was taking her, and I didn't care. I was still pumped up from all the excitement.

"Come on," I said to Stanley, and turned back toward the entrance. "I think saving the world once a night is enough for anyone."

8

"What do you suppose Bud is going to do with Mrs. Crisp?" asked Stanley as we pedaled home.

"Probably hold her hostage," I said happily. "I bet he'll use her to make a bargain with the aliens. If she's one of their leaders, they'll agree to anything to get her back."

For the first time in three days, I felt really happy. The whole alien problem was over, and now I could start to enjoy Halloween. And the best part was, it had been pretty easy. Okay, so Bud had done the actual capturing of Mrs. Crisp. But even the rest of it hadn't been too difficult. If this was the worst the weirdness in Eerie could throw at us, I knew we'd be able to beat it.

"Don't forget," I said to Stanley when we reached our street and pulled up to my garage.

"Tomorrow is Costume Day at school. I say we knock them out with our cool outfits."

"I don't know about that," Stanley said. "I feel kind of weird wearing those masks. They did come from Mrs. Crisp, after all."

"That's what makes it so great," I said. "Who else will have costumes made by a real alien? Think of them as trophies we get for defeating the freaks from outer space."

"Well, when you put it that way," said Stanley slowly, "I guess it would be okay. I mean, even if she is an alien, she did give them to us."

"That's the spirit," I said, punching him in the arm. "Think like an alien hunter."

"I'll see you in the morning," said Stanley as he turned and went toward his house.

I went inside and up to the Secret Spot. I picked up the space helmet Mrs. Crisp had given me, put it on, and stood in front of the mirror. I looked really cool, and I couldn't wait to wear my costume to school the next day. With the aliens out of the way, I was going to have the Halloween of my life.

Walking to school the next morning, Stanley and I got a lot of looks from the people we passed. Mrs. Boothe even screamed when she looked up from picking up her morning paper and saw a space man and a Karakian moon guppy walking toward her.

"Man, this is great," I said to Stanley through my helmet. "These costumes definitely beat anything we've ever been before."

"It's a little hard to see through this thing," said Stanley as he adjusted his mask. "I keep getting the eye holes turned sideways."

"You'll be fine," I told him as we turned onto Main Street and headed for school.

A lot of other kids were dressed up as well, and pretty soon we were surrounded by a pack of mummies, werewolves, witches, pumpkin-headed ghosts, clowns, ballerinas, and other creatures. There were even some other aliens, but none of them had costumes as good as the ones Stanley and I had.

"Hey—who's under there?" asked someone dressed as a snowman. "That's a great spacesuit."

I just nodded in response. I didn't want anyone to know who I was yet. It made everything more fun.

"What a great fish!" exclaimed a cowboy, pointing at Stanley.

"I'm a moon guppy," mumbled Stanley, trying to rearrange his mask. But the cowboy was already gone.

We entered school and went to our classes,

agreeing to meet again at lunchtime to compare notes about the other costumes we saw during the morning.

I headed for Mr. Upshaw's science lab and went inside. The room was filled with kids in costumes, and I took my seat next to someone in a gorilla suit, who nodded at me and offered me a banana. I shook my head no and took out my books.

When Mr. Upshaw walked into the room, everyone gasped. Instead of his usual boring suit and tie, he was wearing a big pink dress and carrying what looked like a wand.

"Good morning, class," he said as he took his place behind the desk. Then, when he saw that we were all staring at him, he said, "What's the matter? Haven't any of you ever seen *The Wizard of Oz*? I'm Glinda the Good Witch. Now, let's get to work."

For the next forty-five minutes, Glinda the Good Witch—I mean, Mr. Upshaw—talked about soil erosion. For the first time all year, science was actually fun, especially when Glinda demonstrated the effects of erosion by having a kid dressed as Godzilla walk all over a model of Tokyo with his big feet.

All my morning classes were like that. Everyone was in the Halloween mood, and each teacher was trying to outdo the next with weird activities. In English, Miss Crandall let us stage our own version of *Romeo and Juliet* where Juliet turns into a vampire and makes Romeo one of the undead. We all agreed that our version was much better than Shakespeare's. Even gym class was okay, mainly because we played basketball while wearing our costumes and I made a basket by knocking a kid dressed as a big bunch of grapes flat on his back.

Then it was time for lunch. I couldn't wait to tell Stanley about my alien-free Halloween morning and find out what kinds of costumes the kids in his grade were wearing. I rushed through the halls to the cafeteria and went inside.

The cheerleaders had taken over one whole end of the cafeteria for their bake sale. The tables were piled with cookies shaped like pumpkins and brownies decorated with candy corn. There were pumpkin pies and pumpkin squares and pumpkin cupcakes, and even a cake shaped like a black cat. Usually the cheerleaders really bug me, but I was in the Halloween mood and decided to buy something from them.

I looked for Stanley at our usual table, but he wasn't there. I scanned the room for him and found him sitting in a corner by himself. I guessed he just didn't want to sit too close to the cheerleaders.

"Hey," I said as I walked over and sat down across from him. "Trying to keep away from the pom pom wavers, huh?"

He didn't say anything. He just cocked his head and looked at me.

"You wouldn't believe the morning I've had," I said, lifting the face plate of my helmet. I took out my sandwich and started to eat. "This place is a zoo today. Boy, do I love Halloween."

I noticed that Stanley wasn't eating anything. He was just sitting there, studying me.

"You forget your lunch?" I asked. "Want part of mine?"

I handed him half of my sandwich and he took it. He put it to his mouth.

"Aren't you going to take off your mask?" I asked.

He shook his head.

"Good for you," I said. "Keep people guessing who you really are."

Stanley took a bite of the sandwich and started to chew.

"Pretty good, isn't it?" I asked. "Dad put a lot of mayo in the tuna fish today."

When he heard me say *fish,* Stanley put down

the rest of the sandwich. He leaned over, and I heard him spit out a mouthful of tuna.

"What's wrong?" I asked him. "You don't like tuna?"

He nodded, but still didn't say anything.

"Tell you what," I said. "I'll go pick us up some of those pumpkin cookies the rah-rahs are selling. I *know* you like cookies."

I got up and walked over to the bake sale, making sure I put my face plate down so no one would see who I was. Not even Kari recognized me as I walked right up to her and pointed to the cookies.

"How many?" asked Kari.

I held up two fingers, and she giggled.

"Ooh, the strong silent type," she said as she handed me the cookies. "I just love a man in uniform. Is that you, Billy Miller?"

I wondered what she would say if I took off my helmet and showed her who was really under the uniform, but I didn't want to blow my cover quite yet. So I just shrugged my shoulders and turned around.

As I walked back to the table, I noticed that the strange codes were showing up on my face plate again. I figured I must have turned on the microchip when I pulled the plate down. Every time I looked at someone, the little letters flowed across my vision. And every time, the word *human* flashed on and off until I looked at someone else.

As I neared our table, I looked at Stanley sitting there. Once again, the code started running by. It was starting to get really irritating, and I couldn't wait to turn it off again once I sat down.

Then the code stopped, and all of a sudden a new word flashed before me. Instead of the familiar *human,* now the screen was flashing something else. In bright red letters, like a neon warning sign, the screen flashed the words *Karakian moon guppy.*

I stopped dead in my tracks. Something had to be wrong with the display. It had never said anything but *human* before. I looked away from Stanley and stared at a girl in a lion suit. The code sped by, and once more the word *human* followed it. Then I looked back at Stanley. I held my breath as the letters and numbers raced around. Then the red light came on, flashing *Karakian moon guppy* at me.

For a moment I thought maybe the helmet was just malfunctioning. After all, it was just a prop from a movie. It wasn't real. The codes it showed me were just nonsense. Now, for some reason, it was behaving oddly.

But every time I looked away from Stanley and stared at someone else, the helmet came up with *human.* And every time I looked back at Stanley, it came up with *Karakian moon guppy.* Since everyone else was dressed in costumes and the helmet knew they were human underneath, I had no choice but to accept what it was saying about Stanley.

Or at least what should have been Stanley. But if the helmet was right, then what I was looking at really *was* a Karakian moon guppy.

"This isn't happening," I said to myself.

"What isn't happening?" asked a voice next to me. "And are you going to eat both of those cookies?"

It was Stanley. He was standing next to me, still wearing his mask. When I looked at him, the helmet said he was human. Which meant that the thing sitting at the lunch table was an alien. A real alien. I groaned.

"No wonder it spit out the tuna," I said. "It was probably one of its relatives."

"What?" asked Stanley. "What's wrong?"

I pointed at the Karakian moon guppy. "Meet the model for your costume," I said.

"Hey," said Stanley. "I thought Mrs. Crisp said this was the only moon guppy mask around."

"It *is* the only mask," I said. "That there is the real thing. It turns out this helmet of mine is a lot more than just a prop from a movie."

Stanley looked harder. "You mean—"

"It's an alien," I said. "And I was just about to give it a cookie."

"I thought we took care of them," Stanley said.

"Apparently not all of them," I replied.

"Are there any more of them around?" asked Stanley, looking nervously to his left and right.

I looked around the cafeteria, and the helmet flashed *human* over and over again.

"Looks like that's the only one," I said.

"What should we do about it?" Stanley asked.

"We shouldn't do anything," I answered. "This is a job for Bud. I say we go find him."

"Wait a minute," said Stanley as I prepared to leave. "We don't want that thing to be suspicious, right? As far as it knows, you still think it's me."

"So?" I said. "You don't think I'm going to go sit with it, do you?"

"I think you should," said Stanley. "That way you can keep an eye on it while I get Bud."

I sighed. "You're right," I admitted. "It's better for us to know where it is. Okay, I'll go back and keep talking to it. You go get Bud. But hurry!"

"I will," said Stanley. "You just keep an eye on that thing."

Stanley left, and I took a deep breath and headed for the lunch table. I sat down across from the Karakian moon guppy, trying to act totally natural.

"Wow," I said. "That line was really killer. Sorry I took so long."

The moon guppy nodded at me, but didn't say anything. I handed it one of the cookies and started eating mine. The alien took a bite and chewed. It seemed to like the cookie, because it didn't spit it out.

"I bet you're getting a lot of compliments on your costume," I said, trying to think of something to talk about.

The alien nodded again, and I smiled and nodded back. I felt like an idiot, and hoped Stanley would hurry up and return with Bud.

"Imagine anyone thinking that aliens really look like that," I said. I hoped I could make the guppy believe I still thought he was Stanley.

The guppy bristled a little when I said that, but then just nodded its head as if it were agreeing with me. I think maybe I offended it, but it seemed to work.

"People will really be surprised when they see who it is under these costumes," I tried, and the guppy nodded wildly.

I just bet you'd like to give us all a surprise, I thought angrily, but I just laughed as though I were talking to my best friend instead of an alien who wanted to make me its slave.

I don't remember what I talked about for the next fifteen minutes while I waited for Stanley and Bud to come back. All I know is that both the alien and I did a lot of nodding. It must have thought I was really stupid, nodding all over the place and never once letting on that I knew that there was anyone but Stanley under that fish face.

Then, finally, I saw Stanley walking through the cafeteria doors. My heart jumped for joy . . . until I realized that he was alone.

"Hey," I said to the alien. "I'm going to go get us some more cookies. You wait here, okay?"

The alien nodded again, and I got up. I practically flew across the cafeteria to get to Stanley.

"Where's Bud?" I asked, almost hysterical.

"He wasn't there," said Stanley. "The other guy who works there said he went out to do something. All I could do was leave a message for him to meet us here as soon as he could."

"Oh, great." I groaned. "That means I have to keep talking to that . . . that . . . thing for who knows how long. I don't think I can wait for Bud."

"Wait for Bud to what?" said Bud, who walked through the door at that very second. "I just got your message."

"You have really, really bad timing," I said. "But I'm glad to see you anyway. We've found another alien."

"Alien?" asked Bud. "Where?"

"It's a Karakian moon guppy," I said, turning around to point across the room to the fishy alien sitting at my table.

But the table was empty.

"I t's gone!" exclaimed stanley when he saw the empty table. "How could it have gotten past us?"

"I don't know," I said, looking around frantically. "It has to be here somewhere."

I scanned the crowd of costumed kids, hoping to catch a glimpse of the Karakian moon guppy. I assumed that it had seen Bud come in and was trying to make its escape. It was probably trying to hide among the swirling mass of moving kids. But everywhere I turned, all I came up with was humans, and finally I had to admit defeat.

"It got out!" I said. "How could it possibly have slipped by us?"

Stanley pointed to the doorway where kids were filing out with their lunch trays.

"It could have snuck through there," he suggested. "We never would have seen it."

"What exactly did you see?" asked Bud, taking off his cap and rubbing the top of his head.

"A Karakian moon guppy," I told him. "It looked just like Stanley's mask."

"Hmm," said Bud thoughtfully. "My guess is that it thought it would blend in with all of these costumes. It probably didn't count on the fact that Stanley would be dressed the same way. I must say, *I'm* surprised to see you dressed as one of those things."

"Mrs. Crisp gave us these costumes," said Stanley. "We didn't know they were really based on actual aliens."

"Really," said Bud. "That's interesting. Very interesting. I bet the aliens were going to use those costumes for some evil plan."

"You're right," I said. "I bet they were going to trick humans into wearing them so that when the attack came, no one would be able to tell who the humans were and who the aliens were. That way everyone would be confused."

"What a good idea," said Bud, as though he were thinking of something else. "I mean, I bet that's it."

"So if Mrs. Crisp is locked up somewhere, then who is this alien, and what is it up to?" Stanley asked Bud.

"Mrs. Crisp *is* locked up somewhere, right?" I added.

"Oh, yes," answered Bud. "She's somewhere very safe. This must be another alien. But don't worry, we'll find it and make sure nothing else happens. You can be sure of that."

"What if it's still around here?" I asked. "What if it's trying to get us because it knows we know its secret?"

"It won't bother you," said Bud. "No offense, but you guys are small time compared to what the aliens want. They're after something bigger. We'll take care of everything. But keep your eyes open, just in case, okay?"

"I guess so," I said. I was a little annoyed that Bud had called us small time, especially after we were the ones who had uncovered the alien plot in the first place.

"Good men," said Bud, clapping us both on the shoulder. "I know I can count on you two. Now I have to get back to the garage. I have a lube job that needs to be done by two, and I'm way behind."

Bud left us standing in the cafeteria and walked away, whistling softly to himself. Stanley and I started to sit down at a table, when I remembered that I had something to ask Bud.

"I'll be right back," I said to Stanley. "Don't go anywhere."

I ran out of the cafeteria and down the hallway, hoping Bud hadn't left the building yet. When I turned the corner, I saw that I was in luck. He was just pushing open the front door.

"Bud!" I yelled, and he turned around.

I started to jog toward him, when something started to roll across the screen of my helmet. At first I ignored it, figuring it was just doing it's usual thing and would flash *human* in a moment. But when I was a few feet away from Bud, I froze. Instead of flashing the familiar word, the red warning light began to blink, and the words *Karakian moon guppy* appeared in front of my eyes.

I stood there in the hallway, staring at Bud's friendly round face as the red warning light flickered on and off like a demented firefly. I couldn't believe what I was seeing.

"What is it, Mitchell?" Bud asked.

"Um," I said, unable to say anything while I was processing the information my helmet was giving me. "Um—I—um . . ."

By this time, I knew that the helmet didn't lie. Bud was an alien, just like the one I'd seen back in the cafeteria. Then, all of a sudden, it all clicked in my brain. Bud *was* the alien I'd been sitting with back in the lunch room! It was the only explanation. He must have been carrying a cloaking device that made him look like Bud. When he saw me talking to Stanley, he just turned the device on and then suddenly appeared as Bud.

As soon as I figured that out, everything that I had believed for the last two days shattered into a billion pieces. All that time, Stanley and I had thought that Bud was the good guy and Mrs. Crisp was the bad guy, so to speak. Now I saw that it had all been a huge mix up. If Bud was an alien, chances were that Mrs. Crisp wasn't an alien at all.

I had to think. But right then I had to make sure Bud didn't know what my helmet could do.

"Mitchell?" asked Bud. "Are you okay?"

"No," I said. "I mean yes. I mean, I just wanted to—um—say thank you for helping us."

Bud smiled, and for a moment I was convinced that I was imagining the whole thing about him being one of the aliens.

"You're welcome," he said. "And just remember, Mitchell, thanks to you and Stanley, Eerie will never be the same."

He waved good-bye and went out the door. I turned and raced back to the cafeteria to find Stanley.

"Did you find Bud?" asked Stanley, who had bought a pumpkin cupcake and was eating it. His face was covered in orange frosting.

"I found out more about Bud than either of us wants to know," I said. "Come on."

"Where are we going?" asked Stanley, cramming what was left of the cupcake into his mouth as I dragged him down the hall.

"To rescue Mrs. Crisp," I said. "We've made a mistake. A big mistake."

As we ran, I explained to Stanley what I'd seen and what I thought was going on.

"They used us," I said. "The aliens used us to get Mrs. Crisp. I don't know why they want her out of the way, but they do. And we handed her to them."

"I am totally confused," said Stanley. "Could you run through it all again?"

"No," I said. "I can't. It's very easy—Bud is an alien; Mrs. Crisp isn't. Mrs. Crisp is probably on our side; Bud probably isn't. So we have to find Mrs. Crisp and find out exactly what is going on here."

"But we don't know where she is," Stanley wailed. "This was a lot easier when I was sitting back there eating a cupcake."

"We're going to the garage," I said. "It's the only place I can think to look."

Stanley and I ran through town until we neared the garage where Bud worked. The garage doors were pulled down, and no one was in sight. There was a sign in the front window reading OUT TO LUNCH.

"I've never heard of a garage being closed for lunch," I said. "Something is definitely weird here."

We went to the back of the garage and approached the same window we'd knocked on before to get Bud's attention. Only this time we didn't want him to hear us, so we walked as quietly as we could. When we reached the window, I peered inside. Through the grimy glass I could make out the interior of Bud's office and the rest of the garage.

"What's there?" asked Stanley impatiently.

"Not much," I said. "He doesn't seem to be around. There's a magazine on the desk and a lot of oily rags thrown around on the floor, but that's it."

As I finished speaking, Bud walked into view. He had been inside the garage, where there was a car up on the inspection rack. He stopped in the doorway and wiped his hands on his overalls. Then he touched something on his chest, and suddenly he wasn't Bud anymore. He was a Karakian moon guppy.

"I knew it!" I crowed. "He *is* an alien."

"I want to see," said Stanley, crowding in next to me.

Bud the alien stretched his arms, as though testing how it felt to be back in his real form.

"I can't believe we were hanging around with that . . . that . . . giant minnow," said Stanley with disgust.

"Shhh. We need to see what he's doing. Maybe it will give us a clue to where Mrs. Crisp is."

But then Bud walked back into the garage bay and out of sight.

"Darn!" I said. "Now we don't know what he's doing."

Then Bud reappeared in his office. Only now he looked like Bud again, and not like a big fish. It gave me the creeps to look at his balding head and think about how he'd pretended to be our friend, when all along he was tricking us.

Stanley and I ducked down so that he wouldn't see us. When we stood up again to take a look, Bud was leaving the garage through the front door.

"Where's he going now?" asked Stanley.

"Beats me," I said. "But we're going inside."

We ran to the door and pulled it open. Luckily, Bud hadn't bothered to lock the garage up, so we were able to get into his office with no trouble.

We started looking around, but there was nothing in the office except the usual garage stuff like calendars and wrenches and cans of motor oil.

"You'd think an alien would have *something* interesting lying around," muttered Stanley as he pawed through a pile of old *Gas Station Monthly* magazines.

"How about these?" I said triumphantly, holding up some things I'd just found in Bud's desk drawer. They were three of the cloaking devices he'd pinned on us the night we'd met him at the train yard.

"Oh, wow," said Stanley. "That's great."

I stuck one pin in my pocket, fastened one on Stanley, and pinned another one on me. Then we touched the activation buttons and looked at each other.

"Hey! You look like a big green lizard," Stanley exclaimed.

"And you're something with nine arms," I told him. "And a tail."

"Perfect," said Stanley. "I've always wanted a tail. Now let's go over to the train depot and see what we can find out there."

Before we left the garage we remembered to switch off the cloaking devices. We didn't want to start a riot or anything on our way there.

After stopping at home to get our bikes, we

rode over to the old train yard as quickly as we could. We activated the cloaking devices before we walked down the hill to the depot, and then we looked for the door. I thought maybe the aliens would have moved it again, but it was in the same place, and within a few seconds Stanley and I were in the heart of the alien station.

"Excuse me," said a big hippo-like creature with a shock of orange hair who bumped into me when I entered. "I'm late for my ship to Los Angeles. I have a meeting with a big Hollywood producer this afternoon."

"Oh," I said, wondering what the creature looked like when its cloaking device made it appear human. I hoped it wasn't one of my favorite actors. "Break a leg."

"The devices seem to be working," said Stanley. "That thing really thought you were another alien."

"So far, so good," I said. "Now let's see what we can find out in this place."

I headed for the stairway that Bud had taken us up before. I figured that was where all of the offices probably were. And anyway, I couldn't see anywhere else to go.

We went up the stairs, and at the top we turned into a long hallway lined with doors. Walking down the hall, we looked into each room, but they were all either empty or just filled with machines or furniture.

"This is useless," complained Stanley when we'd looked into about a dozen rooms. "We could be here forever."

"Just one more," I said as I went to the next door. Looking through the glass in the door, I saw something moving around inside the room—several somethings, actually. They were aliens. One was a Karakian moon guppy, and the other two were these odd purplish blobs that seemed to ooze around the room. Tied to a chair in the middle of the room was Mrs. Crisp.

"Let's try this one more time," the guppy said to Mrs. Crisp in a voice that sounded like Bud's. "Who do you work for, and what do you know about Operation Surprise from the Skies?"

"I won't tell you anything," said Mrs. Crisp.

One of the blobs slid up in front of her and said in a very high voice, "Then we just might have to hurt those two little friends of yours."

"Not Mitchell and Stanley!" said Mrs. Crisp. "They don't know anything about this. For all they know, this isn't even happening."

"Even so," said the other blob in a voice like shattering glass, "if you do not tell us what we want to hear, we will make sure they are the first ones to go."

"They're talking about us!" whispered Stanley. "And Mrs. Crisp is trying to protect us. She *must* be on the good side."

"We have to help her," I said. "We can't let her tell them anything, even if it is to save us."

Mrs. Crisp was sitting with her head down. Then she looked up. "Okay," she said. "I'll tell you who I am. My real name is Agent—"

Before she could say another word, I opened the door and yelled, "There are intruders in the station! You are needed downstairs at once!"

Bud and the two blobs looked at one another, then rushed out of the room.

"Keep an eye on her!" Bud snarled as he passed me. "Don't let her out of your sight."

As soon as the aliens were gone, I ran over to Mrs. Crisp and untied her.

"Come on," I said.

"I'm not going anywhere with you," she said, hitting at me with her hands.

I'd forgotten that, to her, I still looked like a lizard.

"It's me, Mitchell," I said as I deactivated the cloaking device for a moment.

"Mitchell!" said Mrs. Crisp when she saw my face. "But how—"

"Later," I said, reaching into my pocket and

taking out the third cloaking device I'd taken from Bud's desk back at the garage. "Put this on."

Mrs. Crisp pinned the cloaking device to her blouse and turned it on. Instantly she was transformed into a birdlike creature with black and blue feathers.

"A Ulonian grackle," she said, looking down at herself. "Very pretty. But let's get out of this place."

"Before we go, we just want to say that we're really sorry," I said, and Stanley nodded. "We didn't know you were one of the good guys."

"Don't worry about it," said Mrs. Crisp. "I'll explain everything when we're out of here. Now let's go before they figure out that you tricked them."

We ran down the hall and into the main depot. The atmosphere there was as busy as usual, and it was easy for us to slip through the crowd and out the door without being asked for our tickets.

When we were safely away from the depot, we all decloaked, and Mrs. Crisp turned to us.

"I suppose you two deserve an explanation," she said. "I'm very sorry you were dragged into this at all. But now that you have been, you should know what's going on."

"First, let's get something straight," said Stanley. "Is it safe to assume that you are *not* an alien?"

Mrs. Crisp nodded. "Yes," she said. "I'm as

human as the two of you are. You *are* human, aren't you?"

We nodded.

"Good," she said. "Just checking. Anyway, I work for a secret department of the government. We're so secret that almost no one knows we exist."

"What is it called?" I asked.

"We're so secret that we don't even have a name," she said. "We are just called the Department."

"What do you do?"

"We monitor alien activity," said Mrs. Crisp. "Recently, we noticed intense activity centered around Eerie. We'd never seen alien activity here, and we still don't know exactly why they've picked this town to focus on."

"I think we can help you with that one," I said, thinking about the weirdness leak. "But that can wait. What are you doing now?"

"We intercepted information about Operation Surprise from the Skies," said Mrs. Crisp. "I was sent here to find out exactly what it is. The Monster Factory was my cover. What I didn't know was that the aliens were on to me."

"You mean Bud," I said.

Mrs. Crisp nodded. "He didn't know exactly how much I knew, which is why he befriended you. He needed to find out. When he realized that

I knew more than he wanted me to, he used you to set me up."

"Like I said, we're sorry about that," I said. "But what else do you know about Operation Surprise from the Skies?"

"While Bud was interrogating me, he let it slip that the aliens are going to use the parade—my parade—as a distraction while the aliens quietly land and take over."

"Actually, that was our idea," said Stanley. "We didn't think he would use it against us."

"Well, he is," said Mrs. Crisp. "Tonight is the big night. And we have to figure out a way to stop what's going to happen. When I was kidnapped I lost contact with my team, so they aren't aware that everything is going down tonight. It's too late for them to get here, so we have to do this ourselves."

"But we can't stop an entire alien invasion," said Stanley.

There was silence as we all thought about our predicament. The situation seemed hopeless. I looked down from the hill at the town of Eerie resting quietly beneath the gray October sky and thought about aliens taking over.

Then my eyes fell on the broadcast antenna of WERD, and suddenly I knew what we could do.

10

"*T*hat's it!" I exclaimed. "That's the answer to our problem!"

Stanley and Mrs. Crisp looked at each other in confusion.

"What is, dear?" asked Mrs. Crisp.

"The radio station," I said, pointing to the tower. "My dad's radio show."

"You're going to defeat the aliens by playing old music and talking about nothing?" asked Stanley.

"No," I said. "My father is doing that *War of the Worlds* thing on his show tonight. We can get him to warn people about the aliens instead. That way they can't surprise us with an attack."

"Good thinking!" said Mrs. Crisp. "What time is he doing his show?"

"It starts at four-thirty," I told her. "The same time as the parade."

Mrs. Crisp looked at her watch. "That only gives us twenty minutes," she said. "You two run to the station. I'll head back into town and see what I can do about the parade."

"Take Stanley's bike," I told her. "He and I can double on mine. It will be faster that way."

Mrs. Crisp climbed onto Stanley's bike and, after a wobbly start, sped off toward town. Stanley climbed onto the handlebars of my bike, and away we went. It was harder pedaling for two, but once I got going, it was okay. Besides, my adrenaline was really flowing, and I barely felt my legs as I pumped the pedals.

Radio station WERD is on the edge of town, so it wasn't too far away. However, it's also on top of Eerie's highest hill, and getting up it took a lot out of me. By the time I reached the top, I could hardly breathe. I looked at my watch. It was 4:27, three minutes before air time.

"Hurry!" I said to Stanley, staggering for the front doors of the station. I shoved them open and ran into the lobby, where the receptionist looked up at me, startled.

"Mitchell?" she said, as though she didn't recognize me. "Is something wrong?"

"Where's my dad?" I asked, realizing that I was still wearing my Halloween costume and probably looked crazy. "It's an emergency."

"He's in the studio," she said, looking at the blinking red light over the studio door that signaled when someone was inside and on the air. "But you can't—"

"Oh, yes, I can," I said, and ran for the door. I pushed it open and went inside.

There were seven or eight people in the studio, all arranged around a table with microphones on it. My father was sitting in the middle of them. He had a script open in front of him, and he was saying something to the group.

"Okay, we're on in thirty seconds. Bob, make sure you have the sound effects timed exactly right. Greg, when you do the alien voice—"

"Dad!" I yelled, and my father looked up.

"Hey, Mitch," he said, smiling. "I knew you and Stanley couldn't keep away. Come on in. I have parts you guys can read. But hurry up, because—"

"No time, Dad!" I said, running over to the table. "Give me that microphone."

I glanced over at the clock on the wall and saw that in five seconds the show would go on. I flipped on the microphone, and as soon as the green light flashed meaning the airwaves were open, I started talking while my stunned father and his friends stared at me.

"Citizens of Eerie," I said. "This is an emergency broadcast. I repeat, this is an emergency broadcast. You are all in great danger. An alien invasion is about to take place right here in Eerie, and you need to be prepared."

"Wow," I heard my father whisper behind me. "He's a natural. That's even better than the script I wrote. And he really sounds terrified."

All of a sudden, the studio was filled with the sounds of alien ships landing. At first I thought it was really happening. Then I realized that it was just my dad's sound-effects guy. He thought I was just doing the show as planned!

"This is *not* a radio show," I shouted into the microphone, trying to drown out the sound effects. "This is real. In a few minutes, Eerie will be swarming with aliens who want to take over the Earth. They will be disguised, so you have to be very careful."

The room filled with the sounds of people screaming in panic. I looked over at the sound-effects booth, and Bob gave me a big thumbs-up sign, grinning like an idiot.

"Stop!" I shouted at him, but it went out over the air as well. "This isn't a joke. This isn't a stupid radio show. This is the real thing. There really *are* aliens invading Eerie."

"That's great, Mitch," my dad whispered. "Just

great. Keep that up and we'll have the highest-rated show of the year."

It was useless. Everyone thought I was just doing a radio program. In frustration, I clicked the microphone off and jumped up from the table.

"Come on, Stanley," I said. "We have to get into town and help Mrs. Crisp."

"Hey!" my dad yelled as we left the studio. "Where are you going?"

"To save the world!" I shouted back as we ran out the door. "Keep doing the program." Even if the show was a fake, I hoped maybe people would believe it enough to give the aliens some trouble.

The ride back into Eerie went very quickly, mainly because we were riding down the big hill that WERD sat on. All I had to do was lift my feet up, and the bike whizzed down the steep slope. We headed right for Main Street.

"Look out!" shrieked Stanley as we got closer and closer to the center of town. "The parade is starting. You're going to run right into it."

The street was filled with people in all kinds of costumes. There were also a number of floats lining the road. In order to avoid crashing into one of them, I had to slam on the brakes. The bike went into a skid, and Stanley and I screamed as we held on for dear life. Luckily, the bike stopped a few inches away from a kid dressed like a giant bumblebee.

"Hey, watch it!" she said. "You almost wiped me out."

"Sorry about that," I said.

We got off the bike and left it parked by a tree while we went in search of Mrs. Crisp. We checked the Monster Factory first, thinking that she was probably there, trying to contact help of some kind.

Sure enough, she was in there. But there wasn't much she could do. All of her equipment was gone. The storage room was totally empty.

"They came in and stole it," she said, waving her arms around the barren store. "Everything. The aliens took everything. Now there's no way for me to reach the Department."

"This just gets worse and worse," I said. "My dad thought I was acting. You don't have any of your equipment. And we don't know how or when the aliens are landing."

"We do still have *one* thing," said Mrs. Crisp. "We have your space helmet. That will at least help us figure out who's an alien and who isn't. They're sure to be disguising themselves."

"That won't do much good if we can't figure out what they're doing," I said dejectedly.

"It's a start," said Mrs. Crisp. "Now let's get

out there and start hunting some aliens. But first I'd better put on a costume. Otherwise the aliens will spot me in a second."

Mrs. Crisp pulled a costume off the wall and put it on. It was a witch's outfit, with a big black hat and cape. She also put on a fake nose and a long black wig to hide her face. Then we went back outside and joined the festivities. People were parading along Main Street, laughing, waving, and smiling. The sidewalks were lined with spectators, and everywhere I looked I saw masked faces. Some were funny and some were creepy, but it wasn't masks I was interested in. It was aliens.

I pulled down the face plate of my helmet and started scanning the crowd. It was hard to get a fix on anyone because everybody was moving around. But the helmet did its thing, and the word *human* kept flashing on and off in front of my eyes.

"See anything suspicious?" asked Mrs. Crisp.

"Nothing," I said. "Just a bunch of trick-or-treaters having a good time."

We pushed through the crowd, walking in and out of the floats as they rolled along Main Street. Some of the floats were really interesting, and if I hadn't been chasing aliens, I would have liked to have stopped to look at them. But I had a job to do.

All around me people were laughing and having a good time. Some people were handing out candy on the street, and a lot of trick-or-treaters were carrying bags overflowing with goodies. But none of them were aliens.

"Something's wrong," I said when we'd worked our way through most of the parade without finding a single alien. "There should be at least a few creepy outer-space types running around by now. But there isn't a single one."

"There's the float from the garage," said Mrs. Crisp, pointing to a giant pumpkin that was rolling along in front of us with the words EERIE GAS painted on the side. "Is Bud around?"

I looked all around us, but there was no sign of Bud or his alien alter ego. And the guy driving the truck that pulled the giant pumpkin float registered as human on my helmet.

"He's clean," I said, pointing at the driver. "I wonder if he knows who he's working for."

"And where's his boss?" said Mrs. Crisp. "This is getting weirder and weirder."

We'd almost reached the green lawn in front of the town hall. That's where the parade was supposed to end and the party was going to start. Already, there were a few people bobbing for apples and going into the haunted house that the Eerie Scouts had set up.

The floats were all lined up in front of a table where the parade judges sat to review them. The crowd formed around the floats as everyone waited to hear who the winner was going to be.

Mr. Crawford was the head judge, and he was busily walking around each float and writing on a clipboard he carried. After he'd checked out the last entry, he went back to the table and talked to the other judges. A minute later, they all nodded. Then Mr. Crawford walked up to a microphone.

"Excuse me," he said, tapping on the microphone and making a horrible shriek come out of the speakers set up behind him. "Sorry about that. Now, if you'll all listen up, we're ready to announce the winner of the Halloween parade float contest."

Mr. Crawford took a big blue ribbon from the table behind him and held it up. "The grand prize for most original float goes to . . . Eerie Gas and their giant pumpkin!"

The crowd clapped politely, and several people cheered as the driver of the float got out and walked up to accept the award.

"Uh—thanks a lot," he said as he took the ribbon from Mr. Crawford. "This float was really all

Bud's idea, and I wish he were here to accept this award. But he said he had to—um—go do something, so he isn't here."

There was an awkward silence as the man stood there silently, as though he were trying to think of something else to say. Then Mr. Crawford gently pushed the man away from the microphone and started talking again.

"Okay, then," he said. "Well, why don't we move on to—"

Before he could finish, an odd noise filled the air. It was a high-pitched whirring sound, like billions of bees had suddenly flown overhead. Everyone looked around for the source of the commotion.

"It's the pumpkin!" someone shouted, and everyone looked at the float.

Sure enough, something weird was going on with the pumpkin. For one thing, it had started to glow. For another, it was rising up in the air. As we stared at it, the giant pumpkin hovered over our heads, glowing bright orange.

"Oh, no," said Stanley. "I recognize that thing."

"What do you mean?" asked Mrs. Crisp.

"That's no pumpkin," I said, remembering what Stanley and I had seen out the window of the Secret Spot on Sunday night. "That's a spaceship."

No sooner had I said it when the night was lit up by a dozen round orange globes. The Halloween sky was filled with pumpkin spaceships, all of them hovering menacingly over Eerie.

"They must have been there the whole time, hidden by cloaking fields," said Mrs. Crisp. "No wonder we didn't see any aliens running around down here. They were all up there, waiting for the perfect moment to attack."

All around us, people were staring up at the spaceships. I was sure there would be a lot of screaming, followed by a stampede as people rushed away from the aliens. But that's not what happened at all.

"Wow," said a little boy next to me dressed as a ghost. "What a great show."

That started everyone murmuring, and pretty soon people were smiling and pointing to the pumpkins as if they were all just part of the parade.

"That really does deserve first place," said a woman in a cow suit. Then she started to clap, and pretty soon everyone else was clapping, too.

"They don't get it," I said to Mrs. Crisp and Stanley. "They're about to be taken captive by aliens, and they think it's some kind of performance."

The pumpkin that had been on the float moved

until it was in front of the town hall. Then it lowered to the ground and a door opened up. One of the purplish blobs we'd seen interrogating Mrs. Crisp came sliding out.

"People of Eerie," it said in its weird voice. "We have come to take over your town. Prepare for our arrival."

The crowd applauded, thinking the blob was part of the show.

"This is awful." I groaned. "They have no idea what's happening. They think it's all a big play or something."

"That's it!" said Mrs. Crisp.

"Huh?" I said.

"We can use your father's play after all. In *War of the Worlds,* the humans defeat the aliens. That's the part your father should be at right about now. If we play his broadcast over the speakers, then the aliens will think that they're being defeated."

"It's worth a try," I said. "Let's go."

We ran over to the microphone that Mr. Crawford had used, trying not to attract any attention to ourselves. I took the microphone, and we put it next to the speaker of a radio that had been set up to play music. I turned the dial to WERD and turned up the volume. The sound of laser fire filled the air.

"We have a direct hit!" my father's voice boomed from the two speakers on either side of me. "The alien ship is in flames."

There were more sounds of things being fired upon, and the crowd applauded again.

"What great effects," someone said. "This almost feels real."

"There's no need to panic now," my father said. "The people of Eerie are not going to be invaded. We will fight till the end!"

In front of the pumpkin, the purplish blob began moving around in confusion. Even though it couldn't see any fighting, the radio broadcast made it sound like somewhere in Eerie the aliens were being wiped out faster than they could land.

"Take that!" shouted my father, and there was the sound of an alien ship exploding.

The blob took one more look around and slid back into the pumpkin. The door shut, and the ship rose up into the air again. Then, as suddenly as they'd appeared, all of the ships *whooshed* off into the night, and the sky over Eerie was once again filled only with stars. The crowd roared with approval.

"I don't know how they did that, but it was the best show I've ever seen," said a woman behind me. "I hope they do it again next year."

I turned off my dad's broadcast and sighed.

"Did that really work?" I asked Mrs. Crisp.

She nodded. "I think so," she said. "And why not? When *War of the Worlds* first aired, people really thought aliens were attacking. So why shouldn't the aliens think that the people were attacking them this time?"

"But won't they be back when they figure out it was a trick?" asked Stanley.

"Maybe," said Mrs. Crisp. "But by that time I'll be able to get reinforcements, and we'll be ready."

"What about the train depot?" I asked.

"I'm sure it would be cleaned out by the time we could get there," said Mrs. Crisp. "They wouldn't be stupid enough to use it anymore."

"I guess our work is done, then," I said.

Mrs. Crisp smiled and patted me on the back. "At least for now," she said, and cackled her best witch laugh.

EPILOGUE

EPILOGUE

With the aliens gone, the Halloween party went on as planned. Nobody suspected that the spaceships and the purple blob were anything but a fantastic show. Well, except for the poor guy from Eerie Gas. For about an hour afterward he was walking around mumbling to himself, and every so often he would look up at the sky and scratch his head.

"Bud built that thing?" he kept saying. "But he couldn't even rebuild the engine on that '67 Gremlin. Somethin' weird is goin' on here."

Then Mrs. Crisp went up to the confused man and told him that Bud had left a message with her saying that he had to leave town suddenly and was handing over the Eerie Gas business to him. The man's face lit up, and he seemed to forget all about what he'd seen. Then he ran off to join the taffy pull, and that's the last we saw of him that night.

"So what happens now?" I asked Mrs. Crisp as the three of us stood on the lawn, watching the trick-or-treaters and chewing on candy apples being passed around by a pack of goblins.

"Mmmmff," answered Mrs. Crisp, her mouth filled with caramel. "I mean, I go back and make a report to the Department. Then they'll decide if anything more needs to be done here."

"That means you're leaving?" said Stanley sadly. "I was kind of hoping you'd stay around."

"Yeah," I agreed. "It's not like there's anyone else around here who knows how weird things are."

Mrs. Crisp smiled. "Believe me," she said. "I understand how it is being the only one who knows what's going on. Do you think my family knows I work for the Department?"

"They don't know?" said Stanley.

Mrs. Crisp shook her head. "As far as they know, I'm just Grandma. They think I belong to a senior citizens group that takes lots of trips. Right now I'm supposed to be in Vermont looking at the leaves with a lot of other old people."

"Wow, I wonder what my grandma is up to when I'm not around," I said.

"The last time I saw her, she was wrestling a nine-faced Mercurian skink," said Mrs. Crisp, then grinned when she saw my jaw drop.

"Just kidding," she said. "But you never know."

We finished our apples and then walked Mrs. Crisp back to the Monster Factory so she could pick up the last of her things.

"That should do it," she said as she tucked a couple of items into her purse and snapped it shut. The cleanup crew will be through here later to get the heavy stuff. By morning there will be no trace of this place at all. We don't like to leave any tracks."

"I guess we should leave these here," I said, putting my space helmet on the counter next to Stanley's fish head.

Mrs. Crisp looked around. "I don't think it would hurt if you two kept those," she said. "As long as you keep them somewhere safe."

I smiled. "We have just the spot for them," I said.

"Yeah," said Stanley, picking up the guppy head. "The Secret Spot."

"The Secret Spot?" said Mrs. Crisp. "What's that?"

"Just think of it as the Eerie branch office of the Department," I said.

Mrs. Crisp gave us a number where we could contact her if we had any more alien trouble. Then we said good-bye and rode our bikes home. As we wound our way through the streets of

Eerie, I looked at everyone running around having a good time as they knocked on doors and tried to scare one another. I wondered if I would ever be able to do that again, or if being responsible for all of Eerie's weirdness meant never being a normal kid.

When we got to my house, we parked our bikes and went inside. My dad was in the kitchen, telling my mom and Kari about how well his show had gone. When Stanley and I walked in, he jumped up.

"Here's my star of tomorrow now!" he said, putting his arm around me. "Mitch, the guys can't stop talking about what a natural you are. You made the show tonight."

"But I ran out," I said. "Aren't you mad?"

"Mad?" my father said. "How could I be mad? You made it all sound so realistic that we almost believed there was an alien invasion. We just followed your cue."

"I'm glad I could help," I said. I wanted to tell him that he was the one who really saved the day, but I knew I couldn't. He would have to believe that his show had been just another show.

"Well, I guess we'll go upstairs and watch the end of the monster movie marathon," I said. "It's been a long night."

Stanley and I turned to walk out of the kitchen, but my mother stopped us.

"Where's all your Halloween candy?" she asked. "You usually have enough for an army."

"Oh—um—we didn't really have time for trick-or-treating."

"Yeah," said Stanley. "We were kind of busy saving the—"

"Helping a friend," I interrupted. "She needed some help with her party."

My mother smiled. "Well, then," she said, opening a cupboard and pulling out two bags. "I guess it's a good thing I have these."

She handed us each a bag overflowing with all kinds of candy. All of our favorites were in there, from gummy fish to chocolate bars, marshmallow chewies to hot balls.

"Thanks!" Stanley and I said at the same time.

"When your dad told me what a rush you were in to get out of the station, I figured you must have had something important to do. So Kari and I made the rounds for you, just in case," said my mom.

"You guys went trick-or-treating?" I said.

Kari nodded. "I was Little Bo Peep, and Mom was my sheep."

I looked at my mother. "Baa!" she bleated.

"And you guys don't want any of this?" I said.

"It's all yours," said my mother. "I don't think my teeth could handle that much sugar."

"And I already ate the stuff I like," admitted Kari.

"All right," I said to Stanley. "We can still have our Halloween pig-out."

We went up to the Secret Spot, spread out our sleeping bags, and flipped on the television. We were just in time to catch the beginning of the next movie, *It Came from Behind the Moon*. As the action started, I tore the wrapper off a candy bar and took a big bite.

"Finally, this feels like a normal Halloween," I said, and Stanley nodded in agreement, his mouth stuffed with a peanut butter chew.

That was when we both saw the flash of light outside the window. It was a quick burst of orange, and then it was gone.

"Is that what I think it was?" asked Stanley.

I looked at the candy bar in my hand. Then I looked at Stanley and grinned. "Probably," I said. "But let's wait until tomorrow to find out."

Eerie Activities

EERIE HIDDEN SECRETS

Mitchell and Stanley know that in Eerie, Indiana, things are sometimes not quite what they seem on the surface. Take a look at the words themselves, for instance. Mitchell and Stanley have found more than 45 words that can be spelled using only the letters from EERIE INDIANA. Can you beat them at their own game?

Note: No proper nouns or abbreviations allowed.

For answers, see page 154.

EERIE INDIANA

EERIE I. Q.

1. **The population of Eerie, Indiana, is**
   a. 16,661
   c. 10,101
   b. 101
   d. 5,555,555
2. **The owner of the Cable Stop is**
   a. Mrs. Crisp
   c. Ted Tanner
   b. Mr. Crawford
   d. Elvis
3. **How do Marshall and Simon travel through the dimension to contact Mitchell and Stanley?**
   a. through the microwave
   c. the television
   b. by bicycle
   d. bus
4. **Stanley shrinks when _____ gets spilled on him.**
   a. ketchup
   c. green water
   b. diet soda
   d. detergent
5. **For Halloween, Stanley dresses up as**
   a. Elvis
   c. the Loch Ness Monster
   b. a Karakian Moon Guppy
   d. a Space Alien
6. **The local hot dog vendor is**
   a. also a math teacher
   c. Kari, Mitchell's sister
   b. a witch
   d. also a psychiatrist
7. **The new satellite dish gives TV watchers ____new channels to choose from.**
   a. 2000
   c. 21
   b. 10,052
   d. 16,616
8. **Mitchell's mother works at**
   a. the local truck stop
   c. Eerie University
   b. Whatsits, Inc.
   d. B.F. Skinner School
9. **In Eerie, the law of gravity is suspended**
   a. alternate Thursdays
   c. the whole month of June
   b. on Memorial Day
   d. on Stanley's birthday
10. **Stanley's _____ falls through dimensions and lands right on Simon's head.**
    a. high-top sneaker
    c. lunch
    b. backpack
    d. autographed baseball

For answers, see page <u>154</u>.

WORD SCRAMBLES

Ever since the change in dimensions, everything in Eerie is scrambled. After all, it is the center of weirdness for the entire planet. So it's probably no surprise that the most popular feature in the *Eerie Examiner* is the Word Scramble puzzle.

For each puzzle, unscramble the Eerie words, then write down the circled letters and unscramble them to answer the question below. *For answers, see page 155.*

Puzzle One:

HARMLALS (_) _ _ _ _ _ _ _

DRDORFA _ _ _ _(_)_ _

REEEI _ _ _(_)_

AIDNANI _(_)_ _ _ _ _

NYSLATE (_)_ _ _ _ _ _

The circled letters are: _ _ _ _ _ _ _

Question:
The name of Marshall's best friend and next-door neighbor is:_____

Puzzle Two:

DINYS (_)_ _ _ _

RESTNE _ _ _(_)_ _

AHSD (_)_ _ _

RORREFEWAVE _ _ _ _ _ _ _(_)_ _ _

FNOLMAW _ _ _ _ _(_)_

RIAXNEME _ _ _ _ _ _ _(_)

RISKNEN (_)_ _ _ _ _ _

RDGAE (_)_ _ _ _

SELVI _ _ _(_)_

The circled letters are: _ _ _ _ _ _ _ _ _ _

Fill in the blank:
Eerie Indiana is the center of _____ for the entire planet.

151

MORE HIDDEN SECRETS

In the letters below, find twelve things that you'd see in Eerie, Indiana. Circle the answers—across, down, diagonally and backwards! *For answers, see page 156.*

```
L K V Y P D N W E I R D
F A X B F S K I N N E R
R R E E R I R B U K R G
Y I N I S E S A E L V I
E R V H E T H D S L K W
L J L P E I R J N E R I
N C E R U O I D E H D B
A Z C S F Q N Z T C L R
T E K W P R K U R T N U
S D A E L V I S O I K T
N R M B U D N I H M Y U
C F J T S L G H N W P S
```

1. Crawford
2. Eerie
3. Shrinking
4. Mitchell
5. Stanley
6. B.F. Skinner

7. Bud
8. Elvis
9. Weird
10. Secret
11. Hortense
12. Brutus

TWISTED WORDS

Take a strip of paper (about 1/4 inch wide and about 10 inches long). Starting at either end of a pencil, wrap the paper around the pencil diagonally, so most of the pencil is covered by the paper. Put a small piece of tape at each end to hold the paper on the pencil. Now, using another pencil or a pen, write your message along the wrapped pencil. When you remove the tape and unwrap the paper, your message will be impossible to read . . . until your friend wraps it around a pencil that's the same size. Try it!

Eerie Answers

EERIE HIDDEN SECRETS

a	din	in	rained
ad	dine	inane	ran
an	dined	inn	read
and	diner	inner	red
are	dinner	ire	reed
dare	dire	nadir	rein
darn	drain	near	reined
dean	ear	neared	rend
dear	end	need	rid
deer	era	nerd	ride
den	id	nine	rind
die	idea	rain	

EERIE I. Q.

1. a		6. b	
2. c		7. a	
3. c		8. b	
4. d		9. a	
5. b		10. d	

WORD SCRAMBLES

Puzzle One:

HARMLALS   (M) A R S H A L L

DRDORFA   R A D F (O) R D

REEEI   E E R (I) E

AIDNANI   I (N) D I A N A

NYSLATE   (S) T A N L E Y

The circled letters are: **M O I N S**

Question:

The name of Marshall's best friend and next-door neighbor is: **SIMON**

Puzzle Two:

DINYS   (S) Y N D I

RESTNE   E R N (E) S T

AHSD   (D) A S H

RORREFEWAVE   F (O) R E V E R (W) A R E

FNOLMAW   W O L F M A (N)

RIAXNEME   E X A M I N E (R)

RISKNEN   (S) K I N N E R

RDGAE   (E) D G A R

SELVI   E L V (I) S

The circled letters are: **S E D W N R S E I**

Fill in the blank:

Eerie Indiana is the center of **WEIRDNESS** for the entire planet.

MORE HIDDEN SECRETS

```
L K V Y P D N W E I R D
F A X B F S K I N N E R
R R E E R I R B U K R G
Y I N I S E S A E L V I
E R V H E T H D S L K W
L J L P E I R J N E R I
N C E R U O I D E H D B
A Z C S F Q N Z T C L R
T E K W P R K U R T N U
S D A E L V I S O I K T
N R M B U D N I H M Y U
C F J T S L G H N W P S
```

1. Crawford
2. Eerie
3. Shrinking
4. Mitchell
5. Stanley
6. B.F. Skinner

7. Bud
8. Elvis
9. Weird
10. Secret
11. Hortense
12. Brutus